MARKED

My Holiday Taus

Marina Simcoe

To My Captain

Married to Krampus
Copyright © 2020 Marina Simcoe
All rights reserved. No part of this publication may be reproduced, distributed or transmitted in any form or by any means, including photocopying, recording, or other electronic or mechanical methods, without the prior written permission of the author, except in case of brief quotations embodied in critical reviews and certain other non-commercial uses permitted by copyright law. For permission requests, please contact the author.
Marina Simcoe
Marina.Simcoe@Yahoo.com
Facebook/Marina Simcoe Author
This book is a work of fiction. Names, characters, places and incidents are a product of the author's imagination. Locales and public names are used for atmospheric purposes. Any resemblance to actual people, living or dead, or to businesses, companies, events, institutions or locales is completely coincidental.
First Edition
Spelling: English (American)
Story Edit by Amy Q Editing
Copy Editing and Proofreading by Cissell Ink
Married to Krampus is a Science-Fiction Romance. It contains graphic descriptions of intimacy. Intended for mature readers.

Chapter 1

"DAISY! HOW'RE YOU DOING, my baby sister?" The image of Lily's face filled the screen of the ship's communication device I'd gotten permission to use.

"Um... I'm great, actually." I rolled my shoulders back and stretched my neck.

Physically, my muscles still ached and cramped a bit after the five-months long stasis sleep. Thankfully, my journey was almost over. I'd woken up yesterday and only had one more day to spend on this spaceship that was taking me to the country Voran on the planet Neron, the home world of my potential future husband.

Emotionally, I felt even better. Expectant. Elated. Happy, even. Maybe that was the aftereffect of all the drugs and vaccinations I'd received in the past several hours since waking up, but it felt so good to be awake.

"I'm great, Lily." I flicked a strand of my hair back over my shoulder, noting how limp and dull it had become. I should wash and curl my hair before landing tomorrow.

My heart leaped with excitement at the thought of finally meeting Colonel Grevar Velna Kyradus, the man with whom I might spend the rest of my life. Goosebumps rushed down my arms at the thought.

"Are you ready for the landing?" Lily asked.

"So ready! Honestly, I can't wait." I even bounced on the chair a little. Waiting for tomorrow felt very much like Christmas Eve, my favorite time of the year.

I drew in a long breath, calming myself. "How are you doing, Lily? How is everyone?"

"Oh, the usual." She waved me off, swiping a strand of her hair away from her face. Medium reddish-blonde, her hair color was the same as mine. Unlike my long and still matted from sleep locks, however, Lily's was neatly cut and styled into an impeccable bob. "Max and I are working. Kids are in school. Mom and Dad have just left for vacation... But please tell me more about the flight. You're the farthest anyone in our family has ever been, sister."

Actually, I was the farthest *most* people from Earth had been. The first contact with the Voranians from the planet Neron had happened barely a decade ago. There'd been a few visits by political delegations and scientific missions between our planets, but I was the very first regular person traveling that way.

"Five months is a long time to travel," Lily went on.

"Well, I slept through most of it." I laughed.

I'd had the choice to stay awake during the trip. The seven members of the Earth-Neron Liaison Committee, who were traveling with me, remained awake, but they had work to do. I'd just be wandering around the ship for the entire five months, anxious with anticipation for my arrival. I now had less than a day to wait, and I already felt wracked with nerves and excitement.

"We're all so proud of you, Daisy," Lily gushed.

My cheeks warmed with pleasure at hearing that. Normally, Lily had been the pride of the family, and rightfully so. My older sister had gone to college, got a well-paying office job upon graduation, married an amazing guy, and had the two sweetest children.

After a quarter of a century in this world, I hadn't achieved any of that. The bakery where I'd started working straight out of high school closed when its owner, Ms. Goodfellow, retired. I'd moved back in with my parents and worked odd babysitting jobs ever since.

I loved working with children. They had the uncanny ability to make a person forget about their troubles. However, the fact that I had no career, no partner in life, and no place in the world to call my own had been harder to deal with the older I got.

When the application for the Liaison Program had been made public, I applied on a whim. The opportunity to travel to another planet, live among an alien race, and learn a new culture enticed me. Without a boyfriend, a job, or even an apartment, I didn't have much to give up. The position on the application was stated as "Potential Spouse." And frankly, the prospect of an out-of-this-world romance appealed to me, too.

Never in a million years had I thought I'd be the one chosen out of the thousands of applicants. I'd expected a long selection process with several rounds, but the reply came a week after the application submission deadline.

When I saw my name as the selected candidate, it felt like I'd finally achieved something.

"Has he called you yet?" Lily asked.

My smile slipped off.

Colonel Kyradus, my "Potential Spouse," hadn't contacted me at all. There'd been no messages, no calls, no communication, nothing.

I snapped my spine straight and plastered the smile back on my face.

"The Colonel is meeting me upon landing, and I'll be there in less than twenty-four hours, so..."

"Hmm." Lily pursed her lips. "It's rather weird, don't you think, Daisy? Wouldn't a man be eager to talk to his bride? He hasn't even seen you, other than the application picture."

"Well, it's not a typical situation. I'm hardly his bride..."

I wasn't thinking about myself as a bride or a wife yet, though the papers I'd signed were titled, "Marriage Contract."

Voranians' birth rate had historically been hovering at about one girl to ten boys. In ancient times, their families comprised a wife with multiple husbands. Since all the technological advancements and cultural developments had taken place, the Voranian society had eventually moved on to a single partner marriage. Now, a wife only had one husband.

With women being so few, most men never got married. However, every healthy male could have a family on his own. Artificially inseminated, the married females carried the babies of the unmarried males.

Multiple births were a norm. As a result, the Voranians didn't have repopulation problems. Having reached a healthy birth rate in their country, they even ensured the slight population growth required to support their economy.

They weren't interested in human females as breeders. Scientists had determined humans and Voranians weren't genetically compatible to reproduce, anyway. Though, physiologically, the two species could have sex.

Since Voran ended up being populated predominantly by single dads, the role of a human woman would be that of a companion as well as a child caregiver, I imagined.

And that made my heart melt.

The Colonel had two young boys, five-year-old twins, and I was dying to meet them. I had yet to see any images of them.

When I woke up, I'd hoped some kind of communication would have come from the Colonel during my five months of sleep. There had been nothing, and I couldn't help being disappointed.

I hid it from Lily now, smiling wider than ever. There was no need to upset my sister.

"I'll get to meet his entire family soon enough."

Her frown of concern didn't ease.

"I hope Voranians look better in person," she sighed.

"Lily!" I threw my hands up in the air. "You can't hold their appearance against them. For all we know, they're lovely people."

"I know, I know... They're just so scary-looking."

We'd all seen the footage of the official meetings of Voranians with our politicians, and the videos of scientific expeditions to Neron. In addition, I had a photograph of Colonel Kyradus. It was a head shot of him I'd received along with the confirmation letter from the Liaison Committee.

The Colonel was definitely not someone a human would call beautiful. Or handsome. Or even pleasant to look at. In addition to the typical Voranian long horns and scruffy, charcoal fur, his blood-red eyes were, well... "scary-looking." Terrifying, actually.

The moment I first saw his picture, my breath stuck in my throat, and my heart dropped into my stomach. I hid the picture in a kitchen drawer for a while, afraid to keep it in my room or to look at it, especially at night.

Over the course of the few weeks it took me to get ready to leave Earth, however, I'd gotten used to the picture, and even had it as the background photo on my cellphone.

The Colonel's looks meant nothing, I'd decided. Behind terrifying appearances could live the most amazing personalities. Just like many handsome men were major douche bags once you got to know them better. I should know, I'd had my share of pretty boyfriends who'd turned out to be real assholes.

Though, I would've liked to get more pictures or videos of him and his family, the image of the Colonel's flaming red eyes in the picture no longer terrified me.

I'd read and watched everything I could get my hands on about Neron, Voranians, and their culture. Unfortunately, it wasn't much. They had provided me with general information, but I wanted something more personal to give me an idea of the man, his family, and his home that might all become mine, too, one day.

"Lily, I honestly don't care about his looks. I'm sure the Colonel is a nice person, and we'll get alone wonderfully," I said, voicing my wish out loud.

"Daisy, he would have to be a real asshole to *not* get along with you," Lily said in her usual big-sister, no-nonsense tone. "You're a sweetheart, honey. Everyone loves you."

A warm feeling spread through my chest. This was the reassurance I needed. Everything would be fine. Things could always be worked out between people, even if they came from two different planets.

"Aww, Lily. Thank you." I placed my hand next to her face on the screen, missing her and the rest of my family, now. "I love you so much."

"I love you, too, sweetie. And don't worry," she added hurriedly. "You'll do great. You're super easy to get along with. I'll be waiting for your messages, though."

I'd been told I would be able to send written messages to my family on a weekly basis and could have video communication with them on special occasions.

"I'll write every week," I promised.

Lily paused for a moment. Her desire to keep it positive was clearly warring with the big sister's need to warn and protect.

"If anything goes wrong or something doesn't work out..." she started.

"It'll be fine," I assured her. "In the worst-case scenario, I'd just come back to Earth in a year. Either way, it'll be an adventure."

As excited as I'd been to receive the confirmation letter, I had made sure to read the Marriage Contract very carefully before signing it. There was a condition that stated both parties had the right to dissolve the agreement for any reason, after the first full year of the union.

The way I viewed it, this was a year-long employment opportunity on another planet, with an added possibility for romance, which made it that much more exciting.

"Oh, I almost forgot, Daisy." Lily suddenly appeared uncharacteristically flustered. "There is this video that came to your email account here just after you've left. I asked the Committee to forward it to you. It's from the Colonel..."

"A video? From the Colonel?" A new wave of excitement flushed over me. He did send me something, after all. I'd just missed it by having boarded the spaceship already.

"Yes. I can't believe I almost forgot, but it's been five months now, and it slipped my mind... I'm so sorry."

"It's alright." I waved off her apologies. "I can watch it right now, then."

"Yeah, well." She bit her lip again. "Good luck, Daisy. Be careful, okay? And get out of there as soon as you can if anything goes wrong..."

We said our goodbyes, and I tried not to dwell too much on the reasons behind the worry on my sister's face. Instead, I allowed the excitement from finally getting a video to take over.

I quickly logged onto the ship's internal system and found the folder with my name. It contained all the information I had collected on Voran so far. The forwarded video file was also there.

The video took a few moments to load, and I got up from my seat in the ship's communication room to stretch my legs. Glancing at the progress bar from time to time, I paced the small room.

The ship was enormous, with a private cabin for me. My bed proved comfortable enough, but I was looking forward to feeling the ground of a planet under my feet, soon.

I wished I knew more about my destination, too. Waiting for the video to load, I wondered what would be in it.

I hoped this would be the Colonel's home video. The twins' birthday celebration, maybe? Or a family trip? Maybe a dinner with the Colonel and the boys. I would love to see a holiday celebration.

My favorite holiday had always been Christmas. Grandma and I used to bake and decorate early when she'd been alive. I even brought her favorite ornament to Neron with me. Since I would celebrate Christmas away from home this year, I wanted to have something with me that would remind me of my family and of Grandma.

A dinging sound announced the loading of the video was complete, and I rushed back to the screen.

It would be nice to see the Colonel in a casual setting. The one and only picture I had was of him in the dress uniform of the Voranian Army. In it, he was staring straight into the camera. Maybe that was what made his eyes look so exceptionally red? No one turned out good in official photos, right? I had my share of awkward pictures and often used pretty filters when posting photos of myself on social media.

The video opened.

Within seconds, I realized this was not a family celebration. The first image that came up was that of a metal wall. Then, a screeching sound hurt my ears. The wall split open, letting in a bright gush of light.

The landscape of an unknown planet filled the screen—bright red sand and unfamiliar, lush green vegetation.

The camera must have been mounted on someone's body, as the image was unsteady and accompanied by the heavy breathing of the person wearing it. As they turned, a Voranian military aircraft came into view. It appeared to have suffered an accident. It was lying on its side, its shiny metal hull crushed and dented.

A group of what I had first thought were gray boulders on the red ground started moving toward the person with the camera. As they came closer, it became apparent the things were alive.

Approaching the camera, they didn't slow down, menacingly moving closer. Several thin protrusions extended from their large, lumpy bodies. The closest blob of flesh lunged forward, knocking the camera off. It fell to the ground, the image breaking into stripes and dots before disappearing completely.

The next moment, the video resumed from a different angle—a camera from the damaged ship must have turned on. The group of gray blobs attacked a huge Voranian male who looked almost small in comparison.

Bare from the waist up, the Voranian fought fiercely. His fur, slick with sweat and blood, plastered against his bulging muscles as he punched the gray blobs of flesh with his fists and tore at them with his horns.

With a deep growl, he sank his fingers, tipped with long black claws, into one of the blobs attacking him. Baring his teeth in a terrifying grimace, he ripped the flesh apart, drenching himself in the pulsing gush of his enemy's blood.

The camera zoomed in on his face as he tilted his head back and released a deafening roar. The close-up of the Colonel's red eyes left no doubt that it was indeed my "potential spouse" out there, ripping living things to pieces with his bare hands.

Paralyzed by shock, I stared at the screen long after the video had ended.

Was this the man I had to live with? Was that how he behaved at home, too? A shudder ran through me. Was a loving marriage possible with someone like that? Could I even spend a year in his employment?

His poor children...

"Daisy. Are you okay?" A touch to my shoulder brought me out of my troubled thoughts. Nancy, one of the Earth's representatives to the Liaison Committee, gazed at me with concern.

Absorbed by the horrors playing out in the video, I hadn't noticed when she'd entered the room.

"I'm fine..." I mumbled, the nightmarish image of the Colonel's brutal expression frozen in my mind. "I'll be fine... Won't I?"

Chapter 2

"ARE YOU READY, DAISY?" Nancy asked.

We stood at the ship's closed exit, surrounded by the rest of the Earth delegation, all of us waiting for the door to open.

"Sure." I nodded, watching a wide wall section of the ship open and slide down to form a ramp for us to exit.

With sweaty palms, I smoothed the flared skirt of my white polka-dot dress and adjusted the red silk scarf I wore as a headband. I tightly squeezed the handles of the hard-shell, candy-apple-red purse where I kept my Grandma's Christmas ornament.

I'd had a hard time falling asleep last night after watching that video. When I woke up this morning, however, I was able to see things in a new light.

Sending that video was the opposite of a romantic gesture. Obviously, the Colonel wasn't expecting a romance and wanted to make sure I didn't have any such expectations of him. That would also explain why he had not tried to contact me before and showed no interest in getting to know me better. He was looking for a nanny, not a girlfriend. My status of wife would be nothing more than a legality, something to circumvent the law since there was no interplanetary employment agreement between Voranians and humans yet.

The long Marriage Contract that I'd signed covered every political and legal issue of my immigration to Voran, giving few provisions on the actual nature of our union or even my living conditions. It most definitely read like an employment contract.

Adjusting my expectations had calmed me down somewhat. I'd gained a better understanding of my role in the Colonel's household.

The children would be my main and only focus, I'd decided. Thinking about meeting them warmed my heart.

Despite his savage nature, the Colonel still could be a fair employer. I would look after his children for a year for him, learn the new culture, and have a fun interplanetary adventure. Maybe I'd make some new friends.

The fact remained, I was about to disembark on a brand-new planet I'd never been to before. My excitement wouldn't dissipate, no matter what.

"The City of Voran is located in the Northern part of the country," Nancy whispered into my ear as we walked down the ramp into a huge space under a glass dome. "The winter here lasts for nearly six months."

"I know," I whispered back quickly. All this was in the information provided by the Committee. I'd studied it to the last letter. I also knew that summer here lasted just as long as the winter did, with fall and spring being merely a week each.

The city was in the middle of winter right now. Yet I didn't even need a sweater since the ship was connected to the glass dome. The gloomy winter sky stretched above us. However, the air under the glass felt warm. The ground was extensively landscaped with stone garden paths, neat green shrubs, and colorful plants.

I inhaled the fragrant air, saturated with the smell of flowers and wet dirt. It was like landing in an indoor garden. The greenery appeared exceptionally pleasant to the eye after the cold-steel interior of the spaceship that brought me here.

A group of Voranians, about a dozen of them, moved our way along a cobble-stone path. Several in their delegation wore the white-and-gold uniforms of the Liaison Committee, identical to the human representatives who had arrived with me. The rest were dressed in civilian clothes, and I gaped at all the colors and elaborate trim.

In the few pictures of the every-day life in Voran that I'd gotten to see, the clothes definitely attracted attention. Women wore colourful, frilly dresses that reminded me of North American and European fashion in the nineteen fifties. Many Voranian men appeared to like wearing bright colours, too. The civilian suits the delegates wore were embroidered with vines and flowers. Some even had their horns painted with designs in the same colors as their outfits.

A Voranian man dressed in the uniform of the Liaison Committee stepped forward.

"Madam Kyradus, we are so happy to welcome you to the City of Voran," he said.

My translator implant instantly picked up the meaning of his words. However, it took me a moment to realize the man was talking to *me* as he addressed me by the Colonel's name.

"Nice to meet you." I offered him my hand, and he took it with both of his, lowering his head in greeting. I leaned back to make room for his horns. "Please, call me Daisy."

The man blinked, staring at me in confusion.

"I beg your pardon, but that would be against the protocol," he muttered, obviously discomfited.

"Oh…sorry." Breaking local customs and protocols the moment I set foot on the ground had not been my intention. "Carry on then, please."

"Madam Kyradus," the man continued, obviously relieved to use the appropriate moniker. "It's a huge honor to welcome to Voran the spouse of the Leader of the Voranian Army." He bowed again.

I'd only learned recently that Colonel was the highest rank in the Voranian Army, above majors and generals. It had made my future employer that much more intimidating.

"My name is Representative Alcus Hecear." The official raised his head, meeting my gaze with his eyes, the color of lime-green. "I am the Head of the Liaison Committee of Voran."

"Very nice to meet you, Representative Hecear..." I repeated, unsure of what else to say. Meeting high officials of either planet was not something I did often.

The Voranian smiled with another brief bow. He seemed friendly enough, as did the rest of the group. All of them were taller than an average human, their horns adding extra height. Alcus Hecear was clean shaven, but most of the others sported some kind of facial hair—from mustaches, to goatees, to voluminous sideburns, and full beards.

As one of them turned sideways, I glimpsed a long tail with an honest-to-god arrowhead tip, just like a demon's tail was often depicted. A shiver ran down my spine at the comparison.

My gaze slid lower, to their feet. Round and shiny, they weren't feet, but hooves.

Hooves!

I couldn't recall if I'd ever seen a full picture of a Voranian from head to toe, but I certainly had no idea about the hooves. I couldn't stop staring at them, now.

Meeting Voranians in person proved to be a surreal experience.

"...I trust your journey here was pleasant."

I realized Representative Hecear was still talking to me.

"Oh yes, thank you," I mumbled, trying hard not to stare at the Voranians in a way that would be rude, though I feared I'd gone past that point already. "The accommodation on the ship was very comfortable..."

Alcus Hecear introduced each of the Voranians accompanying him. Forcing my gaze up, I made eye contact, politely nodding and smiling at each man as Representative Hecear announced their names and positions.

I couldn't help a glance at their horns, now and then. They sprouted from the sides of their foreheads, slightly curving back and rising about a foot and a half over their heads.

"...Um," I ventured once we'd completed the introductions. "Is Colonel Kyradus not here?" I'd expected him to come to meet me upon my landing, but his name hadn't come up during the introductions.

"The Colonel, unfortunately, is held up in a meeting with Governor Drustan, our Head of State," Representative Hecear explained. "As the Leader of our Army, Colonel Kyradus has a lot of responsibilities—"

"Where is she?" A deep voice thundered suddenly from somewhere, then a large Voranian male energetically stomped from around an intricately shaped shrub and headed toward us.

I took a step back as he came closer. His intense energy seemed to roll ahead of him like a wave, filling in the entire space under the dome.

"Oh, Colonel..." The Representative stumbled out of the newcomer's way as he approached. "The Governor said—"

"The Governor can go fuck himself and his ill-timed meetings." The Colonel obviously held little regard for protocol. He stopped in front of me, giving me a once-over. "Is that her?"

My face burnt as if caught on fire under the intense stare of his flaming red eyes. Judging by how impossibly hot my skin felt, I must look embarrassingly flushed right now. Painfully self-conscious under his scrutiny, I fidgeted with the handles of my purse.

"Um..." I cleared my throat, scrambling for words. I couldn't possibly introduce myself to him using his own name, could I? Screw the protocol. "I'm Daisy..." I said, staring back at him.

Unable to look straight into his eerie eyes, I slid my gaze down his face. His beard was neatly trimmed, shorter than in the picture I had. From this distance, I also noticed that what I'd first thought were painted designs on one of his horns—turned out to be carvings. They wound up in a continuous spiral from the base of his right horn for about two-thirds of its length.

I jerkily stretched my hand to him.

Instead of shaking it the way Representative Hecear had done, the Colonel grabbed my hand in one of his.

"Let's go home." He turned around, tugging me along.

"Oh, Colonel... Sir!" The Representative trotted after us, the clicking of his shiny hooves echoing under the dome. "There are still some formalities left to do..."

"What formalities?" The Colonel glared at him over his shoulder. "Did she get all her shots?"

The question made me feel like a stray being adopted from an animal shelter. My mouth felt too dry for me to protest, however, or even to say anything at all.

"Yes, but..."

The human delegation had congregated closer to us, too.

"Daisy, maybe you would like to spend tonight in our accommodations?" Nancy asked, with concern in her voice.

"We can arrange for a proper ceremony tomorrow morning," Louis, a male representative from Earth, added.

"A ceremony?" The Colonel scowled, tossing him a glare. "What for?"

I kept moving my gaze from him to Nancy then back again, feeling overwhelmed.

"You had her on that ship for months," the Colonel snarled at all of them. "That's more than enough time for quarantine, shots, translator implant surgery or anything else you needed to subject her to." He moved his burning gaze back to me. "As of now, she is mine."

"Mine."

The word sent a shiver down my body, only I couldn't figure out whether it was from dread or thrill. No one had so blatantly claimed me before—in front of the delegations of two worlds, no less.

The unapologetic possessiveness of the Colonel seemed too intense for an employer. And why would I find anything thrilling about his growls?

"Daisy?" Nancy pinned me with a questioning stare.

It appeared they expected *me* to make the call.

The grip of the Colonel's large, warm hand on mine tightened. He didn't appear to be willing to give me up without a fight.

A fight would definitely cause some interplanetary tension. Wouldn't it? I was not a fan of any type of tension. The last thing I wanted would be to become the reason for conflict between the two worlds.

"I'm fine," I said brightly, eager to disperse the expectant silence hanging over us. "I'll be fine," I repeated the same thing I'd been telling myself since last night.

"Your first follow-up interview with the Committee is a week from now," Alcus Hecear reminded.

I nodded silently.

"Call me tomorrow morning." Nancy lowered her head, casting a warning glance the Colonel's way. "Or *any* other time you need to talk."

I nodded again before the Colonel whisked me away, dragging me to the exit.

Surely, it would be safe to spend a night in the house of my *potential husband*? Or future *employer*?

When did it all get so confusing again? It seemed so much clearer just this morning.

Anyway, what was the worst that could happen?

"VORAN IS A BEAUTIFUL city," I said tentatively, sitting next to the Colonel in the two-person aircraft.

He grunted something in response, indistinct to my ear or my translator implant.

I clasped my hands tighter around the handles of the purse in my lap and stared straight ahead.

My mind wasn't really processing the sights of the cityscape that floated past the glass of the aircraft. As we flew above the tallest buildings, the view of the city wasn't much different from what I'd seen in the pictures and videos of Voran—a sprawling cluster of tall buildings topped with rounded glass contraptions. From this distance, the city looked like rows and circles of block towers covered in soap bubbles.

I stared at the view. However, my thoughts remained on my companion. An entire new world lay ahead of me, yet the Colonel had taken over my awareness.

He'd masterfully maneuvered the aircraft out of the parking hangar at the spaceport facility and now was steering it toward his house. At least, I assumed that was where we were going. The Colonel had said nothing about our destination. In fact, ever since he'd dragged me out of the glass dome at the spaceport, he hadn't said a word, replying to all my questions with monosyllables, grunts or nothing at all.

Giving up on small talk for the time being, I slid my gaze sideways, to study the man whose home would be mine, at least for the next year.

One hand on the control panel, the other placed casually on his thigh, his posture seemed relaxed. Obviously, the Colonel wasn't sharing my feelings of awkward tension.

I stared at his hand for a moment. Charcoal-gray fur covered his dark skin. Black claws tipped his fingers. The image of him tearing apart the living thing in the video flashed through my mind again. Thankfully, his claws were shorter and appeared blunt, as if they'd been filed down.

Compared to the flamboyant clothes of the civilian Voranians I'd met at the spaceport, the Colonel's gray uniform looked dull and modest. Its only embellishment was the ornate epaulettes on his wide shoulders and the red-and-gold trim on the sleeves and collar.

After a few moments of the long, unnerving silence between us, I couldn't take it anymore.

"You must have talented artisans in Voran," I said the first thing that entered my mind. "I love the exquisite clothes of Voranians."

I admired the elaborate needlework of the trim edging his sleeve. He followed my gaze, staring at his sleeve for a moment as if seeing it for the first time.

"I guess so." He shrugged.

Well, that was finally a proper reply from him—three whole words.

"Do you know if this was done by hand?" I continued, encouraged by his talking. "Or do you have machines that do this?"

"The clothes?" He tossed an incredulous glance my way, looking genuinely shocked that I would ask *him* anything about textiles.

"Well, the clothes and the trim..." I wished I could just shut up, but he made me nervous. The more out of balance I felt, the stronger my urge to blabber grew. "All of this. Who embroidered this?" I waved my hand over his arm.

"I have no idea." He frowned, raking his fingers through his beard. "Is it something you absolutely need to know?"

"Oh no." I shook my head. "It's not important. I'm just curious."

"Why?" He stared at me.

"Um..." Being put on the spot like that, I couldn't come up with anything other than the truth. "You see, I'm just trying to make small talk here."

He grimaced as if I'd just fed him something sour.

"*Small talk?*"

"Right." I exhaled a shuddered breath, feeling sweat gather in my armpits. Would he be able to smell it? Did Voranians have a sense of smell superior to humans? I couldn't remember.

"'Small talk' translates as 'useless blather,'" he said, flatly. "Why would you waste any time on that?"

"I don't know..." I shifted uneasily. "Maybe, to break the ice? Talking helps people to get to know each other. Does it not?"

Now, he seemed genuinely confused.

"How does learning about the clothes-making process in Voran help you get to know me better?"

I heaved another long breath.

"Well..."

I had nothing.

"I don't know," I gave up.

"There *must* be some better suited questions," he pressed on. "Why don't you just ask me exactly what you want to know?"

And now, I felt idiotic for even opening my mouth at all.

"Okay, um..." I frantically searched my brain. Panic filled me since I couldn't come up with one remotely intelligent thing to ask. Everything seemed either ill-timed or plain stupid.

It wasn't that I didn't have questions. I had at least a million, but now none of them seemed smart or important enough. I was worried about his reaction. So far, he'd acted unimpressed or even severely annoyed by me, which made me even more self-conscious and, at the moment, less able to say anything at all.

"Is there something *you* would like to ask about me? Maybe?" I said, hoping to change the topic.

"No," he replied confidently.

"Nothing?" I blinked, unsure whether I felt surprised or offended, or both, by his complete and utter lack of interest. "Is that why you never contacted me at all? Because you didn't care?"

He shifted in his seat, rolling his shoulders back and stretching his neck.

"The best way to get to know a person is to spend some time with them, in person. I got all the preliminary information I needed from your file."

"Oh, you've read my letter, then?" I asked, with renewed hope.

I was actually really proud of the letter I'd written to accompany my application. It had turned out a bit long, about twelve pages in total. In it, I'd been able to express my hopes and dreams pretty accurately, I thought, as well as give the reader a fairly good idea about myself as a person.

Could I have written it so well, that it left no room for any further questions?

"No. I didn't read the letter," the Colonel replied.

"You didn't?" I breathed out, deflated.

"There was no point." He shrugged again. "You were coming here soon enough, anyway."

I bit my lip. Obviously, he didn't give a rat's ass about my hopes and dreams.

"Listen." I rubbed my forehead, trying to make sense of it all. "Why did you choose me? I've been told there were quite a few candidates."

"A lot," he huffed, grumpily. "Thousands."

"Why *me* then?"

He fiddled with some buttons on the control panel. It didn't result in any visible changes to the course of our aircraft.

"I liked your picture," he said after a minute or two.

"That's it? Just the picture?"

The instructions stated that the application photo had to be unaltered. I couldn't add a pretty filter to it. That picture was all me, unembellished, save for some light makeup.

I'd been called "pretty," but realistically, there were a million better-looking women out there—taller, slimmer, with glowing skin. I simply couldn't have been the most beautiful girl out of thousands.

"What did you like about my picture?"

"It was bright," he explained.

"Bright?"

He nodded. "Your clothes reminded me of the women of Voran. And your hair matched your outfit."

I thought back to what I was wearing in that picture—a sunflower-print dress with a frilly skirt and a green headband. The dress made me feel happy, and I'd thought the hairband looked nice in my reddish hair. Apparently, the outfit turned out *bright* enough to attract the Colonel's attention.

"So, you've chosen your potential future life-partner based on nothing but her clothes and hair color?" I stared at him, flabbergasted. Even if he just wanted a nanny for his children, shouldn't there have been a more complicated selection process? Either way, he was choosing a person to spend at least a year with, under the same roof?

Talk about leaving it to chance.

The Colonel must have seen my bewilderment.

"How would *you* choose in my place?" He glanced at me with a flash of curiosity in his eyes.

"Based on personality, of course," I replied quickly. "I'd love to know the person's likes and dislikes. There are special compatibility tests—"

"Is that how marriages happen on Earth?" he interrupted. "By utilising tests?"

"Well, not exactly. Though the dating apps and agencies use some kind of formula, I believe."

"And how does it work out for humans? How strong are your marriages?"

"Well it works well for some couples, for *most* even. The divorce rate on Earth is somewhere between forty and fifty percent..."

"What?" He huffed. "Your tests and formulas aren't that great then, are they?"

"What is the divorce rate in Voran?"

He lifted a bushy eyebrow.

"Only one in ten men in Voran gets a chance to have a wife," he said slowly, staring at me intently. "One wife. One chance at marriage. Every husband would do anything to keep his wife. Absolutely anything. Divorce is so rare in our country, it's practically non-existent."

I dreaded to clarify what exactly he meant by "would do anything." It could be as in "giving her *anything* she desires to remain happy in marriage," or "doing *anything* possible to physically keep his wife, including tying her up in the basement."

"What if..." I started carefully. "Sometimes things don't work out between two people, you know."

"There is always a way to work things out," he said, dismissing me confidently. His tone left zero chance for arguing. So, I didn't.

Instead, I stared ahead through the glass of the spacecraft again.

"Listen," he said after a while, betraying that he kept thinking about the topic of our conversation even after we'd fallen silent. "My time was limited," he explained. "They gave me thousands of pictures of alien women to choose just one. Yours stood out. And that was it."

Chapter 3

"THIS IS HOME." THE Colonel tipped his beard at the cluster of glass domes and spheres on top of a skyscraper.

"The entire thing?" I leaned closer to the glass of the aircraft for a better look.

The building was so tall, I couldn't see the street below as we hovered near its top. Glass bubbles covered its walls, as if they had been sprayed with foam. The bubbles were the glass-enclosed patios and balconies of various sizes.

The Colonel watched me closely.

"No. The building isn't mine," he said. "I occupy the top three floors only."

"Only?" I exhaled a laugh. "Your place must be the size of an amphitheatre."

The main dome alone seemed large enough to enclose a coliseum. Several others surrounded it, only slightly smaller than the first.

"It's...breathtaking." I stared in awe at the glass glimmering under the late afternoon sun of Neron as the Colonel maneuvered the aircraft closer to the nearest dome.

The glass slid open, letting the aircraft glide inside. It landed on a green platform covered with a neatly trimmed grass. The side panels of the aircraft lifted, and I climbed out. The kitten heels of my Mary Janes sank into the lush indoor lawn, so unusual to see under the paling light of the setting winter sun.

"Is this real?" I turned to the Colonel who was walking around the aircraft to me.

"The grass? Yes. It grows year round, just like the rest of the plants." He gestured at the planters lining the walls and the hanging baskets dripping with garlands of flowers.

"What a gorgeous patio." I slowly turned around, taking in the luscious greenery generously sprinkled with the bright colors of flowers. "It would be so lovely to have tea here in the morning."

"You want to have breakfast in the garage?" The Colonel lifted an eyebrow at me.

A garage?

Of course. Where else would he park his vehicle?

"Well, it's the prettiest garage I've ever seen..." I mumbled.

He kept making me feel like a complete idiot. How was I supposed to know that live grass and gorgeous flowers belong in a parking garage in Voran?

"There is an actual breakfast patio on the other side of this floor." The Colonel led me to a set of opaque glass doors that slid open as we approached. "In the morning, the view is better there than here."

I had no chance to reply. My breath caught in my throat from delight when we entered the next room.

It was perfectly round with a checkered tile floor and a ceiling so high, I had to tilt my head all the way back to see the glass hemisphere of the skylight. Green and yellow plants grew everywhere. Vines hung from the ceiling, draped along the walls, and climbed up trellises. Some of them bloomed with large, vivid flowers, adding splashes of color. A fresh, sweet fragrance wafted through the air.

"Oh, my goodness..." I exhaled in awe.

Pressing my purse to my chest, I strolled around the room, admiring its beauty.

"Do you like it?" The Colonel asked.

His thick eyebrows drew into a frown, though I didn't believe he was angry with me at the moment. He just didn't seem to have many facial expressions, other than frowns of different depths. It was unbelievable that a grumpy man like him would live in a place resembling a paradise.

I couldn't care less about his moodiness, right now. This place was too beautiful to worry about such things. Spreading my arms out, the purse with the ornament clutched in my hand, I took a twirl.

"Like it? I love it!" I couldn't help a soft laugh. "This is gorgeous. A beautiful summer in the middle of winter."

I faced the Colonel, catching my breath.

"You must be an amazing gardener," I gushed, happy to have finally found something redeeming about this man.

He folded his arms across his expansive chest.

"Me? No, this is all Omni's work."

"Omni?" I glanced around for someone with that name.

A whirring sound behind me made me spin around. An object rolled from the opposite door. It was a frame with a screen mounted on a tall stick attached to a short platform on wheels.

"Greetings, Madam Kyradus," a soothing mechanical voice sounded from the softly glowing screen. "Welcome to the household of the Colonel Grevar Velna Kyradus. I am the Artificial Intelligence housekeeping system or 'the house AI' for short. But you can call me Omni."

"Hi Omni." I dipped my head in greeting, since the unit had no hands to shake. "It's very nice to meet you."

With no hands, I wondered how the robot could do anything around here at all, not to mention create and maintain this luscious indoor garden.

"I trust your journey was enjoyable?" Omni continued. "We have received your luggage from the spaceport. I've taken the liberty of taking it up to your room and unpacking."

"Oh, really? Thank you..."

"Would you like me to take this up as well?" The image of the purse in my hands appeared on the screen.

I pressed the purse to my chest, unsure if I was ready to part with it yet, even for a little while.

"Or would you like me to place it near your chair while you're having dinner?"

Insisting on holding onto the purse at this point would make me look like a toddler who refused to give up her favorite toy. The Colonel already seemed to have a less-than-stellar opinion about me.

"No, it's fine. You can take it." I stretched the purse toward Omni, wondering how the screen could take anything anywhere.

With a swish of air against my face, a small silver drone appeared seemingly out of nowhere.

"Could you hang the purse on the hook, please?" Omni instructed.

I did as I'd been told, carefully hanging the purse on a chrome hook extending from the drone. It took off toward a winding staircase that circled the entire room spiraling upwards.

"Carefully, please," I begged, watching the purse with my grandma's ornament fly away. "It's fragile." That was the reason why I didn't leave it with the rest of my luggage, carrying it all the way here myself instead.

"There is absolutely nothing to worry about," Omni assured me. "All my units boast extreme precision of movements.

"Is dinner ready?" the Colonel barked, holding a short wide glass in his hand. He had snagged a drink from somewhere.

"Yes. Follow me to the dining room, please." Omni rolled back to the glass doors he'd come from. The Colonel and I followed.

"Do you drink alcohol?" the Colonel asked me on the way.

I couldn't tell by his tone whether he was simply enquiring before offering me a drink or was getting ready to judge my choices.

Once again, I decided to go with the truth. "Yes, I do."

"Which drink do you prefer?" His tone was gruff as usual but didn't appear judgmental.

"Wine," I said, and added, "If you have something like it on Neron?"

We entered an oval space with a large, glass table in the middle. Just like the room before, this one had a tall clear dome for a ceiling. The entire space also burst with plants and colors everywhere. Even the ornate chandelier hanging over the table served as a lattice for climbing vines. Their red and orange flowers were nearly as bright as its lights.

A drone flew my way with a tall glass of purple liquid clasped in one of its chrome pincers.

"Tell me what you think about this one." The Colonel gestured at the glass as I carefully took it from the drone. "It was gifted to me for a special occasion last year."

"Thank you." I took a small sip and gasped as the purple liquid burned my tongue. The burn, however, was quickly soothed by a fresh, mildly sweet aftertaste. "It's a little strong, I think..."

My knowledge about wine was limited mostly to its color—red or white. I liked drinking it sometimes and didn't need to know much about it to enjoy it.

I glanced up at the Colonel, who watched me intently with unreadable expression.

"It's lovely," I added, just in case.

He nodded, setting his drink down to pull the chair from the table for me. His gallant gesture came as a surprise. Until now, the Colonel hadn't done as much as opening a door for me. But then again, the doors had opened on their own everywhere around here.

"Thank you." I sat down.

A cart rolled in from yet another door to the side as the Colonel took his seat across from me, on the other end of the table. Two drones placed two trays in front of us. They looked like chess boards; small amounts of different foods filled the square indentations.

No matter how nervous the Colonel made me feel, I was starving.

"This looks so good." I ventured another burning sip of wine then lifted a narrow utensil from the table. "Have the children eaten already?"

I wondered where the twins could be, hoping to meet them sooner rather than later. Besides, the presence of children always helped me relax in most awkward of situations.

"The children?" He glanced up at me from his plate.

"Yes. The boys." I popped a small cluster of yellow balls in my mouth. They melted on my tongue with a creamy taste of butter and cheese. "What are their names? I couldn't find that anywhere on the information provided to me."

"My sons' names are Olvar Shula Kyradus and Zun Shula Kyradus," he said with obvious pride.

"Olvar and Zun? Those are beautiful names."

"I chose them." He tossed a piece of food from his plate into his mouth, bypassing the use of the utensil. "Olvar means 'fierce' in Voranian, and Zun stands for 'the victorious one.' I hope they will grow into men who do those names justice."

"I hope they do..." With the hook-like utensil, I fished out a round piece of something else from my plate and took a tentative bite. It had the crisp texture of a watermelon with a tart, savoury taste. "Where are the boys now?"

"In school."

It seemed to be a little too late in the day for five-year-olds to still be in school. But then, this wasn't Earth. I had to expect things to be different.

I tried a small cube from another square indentation. This one turned out to be a piece of cured meat.

"When will they come home?" I asked as soon as I chewed and swallowed the meat.

The Colonel was polishing his food off the tray rather quickly.

"In about three years and four months," he said.

The utensil dropped out of my hand, clinking against the tray on its way down to the table.

"Three years?" I gaped at him, hoping I'd heard him wrong.

"Yes. They are at the Military Academy. The term for full-time studies there is nine years," he explained calmly.

"Military Academy for five-year-olds?" I tried to keep judgment out of my voice. After all, I was on a different planet in a different culture...

It proved too hard, though, to force a neutral expression. I was certain the shock I felt was now splattered all over my face.

"Yes," the Colonel confirmed. "A military focused education has been selected as the most suitable direction for my children."

"Selected by whom?"

"Myself, with the assistance of aptitude testing conducted by The Ministry of Children's Education and Wellbeing."

"How do you determine aptitude in a five-year-old?" I left the utensil where it lay, no longer feeling that hungry.

He stared at me.

"Why a *five-year-old?* My sons have been at the Academy from birth."

My eyebrows must have shot up to my hairline as I stared at him in astonishment. All my thoughts came to a complete stop for a moment.

"How could you possibly teach military tactics to a newborn? I assume that's what's taught at the Military Academy?"

"Right," he confirmed. "Military tactics are a part of the curriculum. Of course, the lessons don't start until later. Newborns don't sit in classes."

"Well, that's good. Since, you know, *sitting* would be difficult for someone who can't even hold up his own head."

He peered at me for a moment, as if trying to decipher the meaning behind my tone. There had definitely been a hefty dose of sarcasm in my voice. My resolve to be open-minded and accepting of the other culture had been proving increasingly difficult to maintain the more he spoke.

"Have your children ever been here, in their family home?"

"On a few occasions," he replied flatly, his expression guarded.

"So, you don't get to see them, at all, then?" I pressed on.

He shifted in his seat, leaning all the way back.

"I see them once or twice a month," he said slowly, "but I track their academic progress daily. I also check their health reports every morning."

"Well, tracking their blood pressure and progress in math doesn't exactly substitute for actually *seeing* them, does it?"

He narrowed his eyes at me then suddenly shoved his plate aside with force.

"Are you criticizing the way I'm raising my children?"

The fading glimmer of the sunset, aided by the soft light from the chandelier, made his red eyes appear to glow against the dark gray of his face. I sensed his displeasure hanging in the air, thick and smothering like a wool blanket. It was terrifying.

I sucked in a breath. My problem was that I could never keep my mouth shut even when it was obviously to my benefit. My tongue often ran faster than my thoughts.

"Not really," I retorted. "I can't criticize how you're raising your children because you're not exactly the one *raising* them, are you? From birth, they've been spending their days with someone else. What does 'having a father' even mean to them?"

"That's enough!" He slammed his hand on the table, making me and the dishes jump. "You've been in Voran for less than a day, and you're telling me how to run my household?"

Too late, I realized I'd gone too far.

"I'm sorry. It came out wrong," I mumbled, scrunching my skirt in my hands. "I definitely wasn't trying to sound disrespectful."

"Well, you've failed at that."

The scorn in his voice made me wish I could just fall through the floor and hide in whatever room was on the level below.

I refused to meet his frightening eyes.

"Maybe, I should just call it a night. I'm still rather tired, with the long flight and stuff..." I let my voice trail off.

My appetite was completely gone. All I wanted was to get out of this room and away from the Colonel.

"Omni will show you the way to the bedroom," he muttered, shoving his chair away from the table.

Chapter 4

THE DINNER HAD GONE badly. Horribly. Much, much worse than I could have expected. With a gruff, grumpy man like the Colonel, one could've suspected things might not go smoothly. The dinner disaster, however, was all my fault. Wasn't it?

The wise thing to do when coming to a stranger's house—especially, the one located on a different planet—would be to stay quiet, listen, and observe first, learn the new culture as I had fully intended to do.

Nope, I had to open my big mouth and spew my freaking opinions left, right, and center...without being asked for any of them. The wellbeing of children had always been a sore topic for me, and I just couldn't stay quiet.

Now, the already awkward situation had become that much more difficult.

Distraught, I wasn't paying much attention where I was going, following the Omni drone up the wide, winding staircase.

When the set of opaque white double doors opened into a huge round room topped with a glass hemisphere, I stopped in my tracks, frozen in awe once again.

"Is this..."

"Your bedroom." Another screen on a stick rolled my way.

Streaked with the fading colors of the dying sunset, the sky above us was already studded with stars on the darkening edge. A large round bed stood in the middle of the room. Supported by two ornate poles that rose from the floor, a lattice canopy hovered over it draped in live flower garlands. The same light fragrance drifted through the air, filling the room, which appeared to be created by fairies.

"This is just... Omni, this place is simply magical," I admitted.

"Oh, thank you, Madam Kyradus."

The sound of the Colonel's name made me wince.

"Could you call me Daisy, please?"

"Absolutely. I can call you any name you wish. Please, let Colonel Kyradus know that you would like me reprogrammed."

"So, you can't call me Daisy just like that? Without his permission?"

"No. I have been specifically programmed to address you as Madam Kyradus."

The Colonel must like hearing his name a lot.

"Alright then. Madam it is, but just for tonight." I made a mental note to talk about this with both the Colonel and the Liaison Committee. It made no sense for me to be called and treated as his wife if we weren't even in a relationship.

I didn't want to give up after just one dinner, as disastrous as it'd been. A first impression was important, but it wasn't everything. Maybe tomorrow we could find a way to work on this together?

Except that the Colonel hadn't shown any intentions to work on anything with me. I hadn't caught a hint of any romantic feelings from him, not a trace of a desire to build some understanding between us. Of course, my judgy rhetoric didn't help the matter, either.

The way things were going, I didn't think any kind of a relationship would ever be possible between us, not even that of an employee and an employer. And with the children not being here, I had no idea what my true purpose in this house could be.

The thoughts pounding in my skull made my head spin. Worry proved exhausting. I stifled a yawn. It wasn't that late in the night yet, but I felt tired.

"You said you've unpacked my things?" I asked Omni.

"Yes. This way please."

The robot rolled behind a planter with a tall lattice covered in vines. It served as a screen, hiding an arched entryway into a large room, which I recognized as a humongous closet.

"Your bathroom is this way." An arrow pointing to the right appeared on Omni's screen. "I've added your clothes to the rest."

"The rest?" I stared at the rows upon rows of hangers lining the walls from the floor to the rounded skylight in the ceiling.

A white, round couch stood in the middle of the colorful rug on the floor. Shelves of shoes, all shaped for human feet, surrounded it.

"Whose clothes are these?" I asked, admiring the bright fabrics that shimmered under the strings of lights intertwined with flower garlands under the ceiling.

"Yours," Omni replied. "The Colonel ordered them as soon as your sizes had been confirmed."

"So, he didn't bother to write a single word to me, but he made sure to obtain my dress size?"

"And shoe size, too," Omni added, matter-of-factly. "As the head of the Voranian Army, the Colonel attends a number of high-profile public events and social functions. As his wife, you will be accompanying him. It is important you're dressed appropriately."

"Right. The Colonel is pretty high up in the ranks, isn't he?"

I slid my hand along the soft, glistening material of the clothes on the hangers. Maybe that was the purpose of my being here? The Colonel needed a female escort to formal galas and such. If so, he'd made a huge mistake by choosing me. Mingling with high society was not one of my strengths. He would have known that had he read that letter I wrote.

"Colonel Kyradus currently holds the highest rank in the Voranian Army. He was promoted just over a year ago, after successfully leading the operation that ended the *fescods'* invasion in Voran."

"*Fescods?*"

"The semi-intelligent species from the planet Tragul. They had almost entirely occupied their planet, then invaded Neron by landing in Voran eleven years and three months ago. The Colonel's actions on Tragul weakened the *fescod* forces enough to withdraw from Neron entirely."

An image of the space blob, identical to those attacking the Colonel in the video he'd sent to me, appeared on Omni's screen.

"*Fescods*," Omni said in a somber voice. "They caused a long and devastating war in Voran. The Colonel's heroic actions last year ultimately led to our victory."

"Wow," I gasped softly, rather impressed. "The Colonel is not just the Army Commander but also a war hero. So many details were not included in the information package I received from the Committee."

"The Committee shared only the basic facts. However, when your request for more information was received, the Colonel ordered me to send the recording of his moment of glory. Not sure if the video reached you, as we were told you had already left for Neron by then."

"It did reach me." I sat down on the round couch in the middle of the closet room. "I watched it on the spaceship, shortly before my arrival here."

The video that terrified me was apparently that of the Colonel's "moment of glory." It must be his way of telling me more about himself, not to intentionally scare me away. Though, a brief message to accompany the video would've been very useful at that time.

My headache had only intensified after all of this.

"I'll think about all of it tomorrow, Omni. I really would love to go to sleep, right now."

"Absolutely." Omni's agreeable voice flowed smoothly. "Good night and pleasant dreams, Madam Kyradus. I'm shutting off this unit now, but if you need anything at all, just say my name."

The stick rolled to the charging base by the wall, then the screen went black.

GREVAR

Fully unbuttoning his uniform coat, he leaned back in his chair, gesturing to the drone for another drink. He rarely drank hard liquor on a week night, but today warranted it.

The privilege of being the first to acquire a human wife had been bestowed upon him by the Governor of Voran. Deep inside, Grevar suspected that Governor Ashir Kaeya Drustan had wished to marry him off simply to keep his attention away from his own wife, Shula. Not that there was anything to worry about. Ever since Shula had chosen Ashir over Grevar, they had been nothing more than friends.

In public opinion, as the decorated war hero and the newly promoted Colonel, he was a logical choice to be the first Voranian to marry a human. It was a great honor he could not refuse.

Not that he wanted to refuse it, of course.

Having a wife was a rare thing in Voran. Artificial insemination allowed a man to have his own family. However, many would be delighted to have a wife in addition to children if given a chance.

That said, Grevar hadn't exactly burst with delight when he'd been informed about the honor bestowed on him. His wife would be a foreigner, an odd-looking alien from a newly discovered planet. There'd be cultural and other differences to overcome. Despite that, he had been looking forward to her arrival.

From the moment he had accepted this marriage, nothing could be changed. Instead of trying to contact his new bride, he'd chosen to wait until he saw her in person. So much could be lost in translation during communication by mail or video feed.

He had chosen Daisy from a stack of pictures dumped on his desk at work one fine morning. There was not enough time in his busy life to even try to go through all of them, not to mention to give any careful consideration to each of them.

All the women in the pictures seemed very much the same to him. Their skin shades varied from beige to dark brown, and their hair colors ranged from pale yellow to black, but those were the only differences, and they meant little to him. None of his potential brides had any horns or fur. And all had looked equally strange with their dull human eyes—alien.

He had expected some complications. Everything about tonight, however, had proven challenging and overwhelming.

Heaving a long breath, he took a big swig from his freshly refilled glass.

Unfortunately, it hadn't been possible to tell from the picture alone how much of a chatterbox his new wife would turn out to be. His head pounded with the ache from her blabbering.

Of course, having anyone at all around here would be a challenge. The most noise he usually had to endure in his home had been the subtle dripping of the irrigation system watering the plants or the whirring of the numerous Omni devices, or the noise of the entertainment system every now and then when he watched the news. That was about it.

Having a chatty woman living under the same roof with him would be an adjustment. Though, maybe not necessarily an entirely unpleasant one.

He liked the expression of delight on her face when she had first entered his home. It reminded him of that happy smile she had in her application picture—bright and full of wonder.

Her voice, melodious and pleasant, wouldn't be too hard to get used to, either. Even if she continued to talk as much as she did, he could see himself being able to tune her out, let her voice blend with the trickling of the irrigation system in the background. As long as she didn't expect him to reply to her every statement, they should be fine.

Hopefully, she'd also *try* harder not to say the insulting things she'd said tonight. He had a thick enough skin and wasn't easily insulted. However, criticism about his children and the way he was raising them was not something he took lightly. Thankfully, she truly seemed sorry when she realized she'd said too much.

This was a new world for her, after all. How well she'd do in it would largely depend on her ability to learn.

The image of her rose in his mind again.

Looking straight at her face had been the most difficult. The lack of horns disturbed him. Staring at her smooth forehead, he couldn't even pretend that she'd suffered some accident resulting in the loss of her horns.

Thankfully, the rest of her didn't seem so bad. There even were some things he really enjoyed about her.

She left a cloud of flowery fragrance wherever she went, a little strong but not unpleasant.

He liked her bright orange-yellow hair. Its sunshine color reminded him of a summer morning. There was also cheerful energy in the way her thick curls bounced when she tossed her head.

Her taste in clothes appealed to him, too. He liked how well the pretty dress she wore hugged the curves of her body.

And he absolutely, positively liked her curves.

The memory of the rounded tops of her breasts swelling above the deep neckline of her dress sent a wave of heat to his groin. He didn't even mind that she had not a shred of fur on her chest.

In fact, he wished to see more of her, without that dress.

That was encouraging. As her husband, he had to bed his wife—it was his duty. Having physical attraction for her made things much easier.

He finished his drink in one gulp and shrugged his army coat off. Standing up, he stretched his back, letting the desire roll through him. His cock pushed urgently against his pants, his skin prickled with anticipation under his fur.

It'd been years since he'd held a woman in his arms. Back then, he'd let her into his heart and his bed, but she'd ended up choosing another man over him.

Now, he was lucky enough to have another woman waiting for him in his bed. Warm excitement coursed through his veins at the thought that she was *his* already—his wife.

It was time to go to bed.

I FOUND MY COTTON EYELET nightshirt hanging on the rack with the garments I'd first mistaken for evening gowns. Taking one off the hanger, I realized this must be a night dress. A pretty scandalous one, too. Without any lining, the sheer material would leave nothing to the imagination.

The silky, shimmering fabric reminded me of dragonfly wings. I slid my hand down the marvelous garment, wondering how it would feel to wear it.

There was no harm in trying it, was there?

Getting out of my dress and underwear, I put the gorgeous nightgown on. Held only by a pair of hair-thin shoulder straps, it draped all the way to the floor.

Logic told me that there must be a mirror in the closet somewhere, but I couldn't find it. I remembered, however, seeing a wide dresser with a large, round mirror over it in the bedroom.

Kicking my shoes off, I padded out of the closet.

My own reflection in the dresser's mirror took my breath away. It looked as if my body was wrapped in a magical shimmer—for that was all this fabric was. Not a solid material but simply a reflection of light. It streamed down my curves like a waterfall, making my rather ordinary body appear as something out of this world.

"This is too fine to just wear to bed," I murmured, twirling in front of a mirror.

The diaphanous skirt fluttered around my hips like a kaleidoscope of butterflies...or night faeries with iridescent wings...

Suddenly, the doors to the bedroom slid wide open, and the Colonel barged in.

His gray uniform coat was gone, and he was unbuttoning his white shirt as he entered. He stopped in his tracks, glaring at me.

I squeaked in shock, trying to cover all my naughty bits at once, which wasn't easy because of the size of my breasts. Each needed an entire hand to be somewhat concealed. Being extremely flustered and therefore painfully uncoordinated didn't help. Never before had I felt so completely naked when wearing a floor-length garment.

The Colonel's eyes appeared to catch on fire at the sight of me. Lowering his head, he ripped his shirt off and stomped my way.

"Oh, no..." I whimpered, retreating until my backside hit the dresser.

The atmosphere in the cheerful, flowery room changed, as if the storm had moved into a sunny meadow. The Colonel took over the space and all my senses at once. Like a huge cloud coming over the sun, his mere presence had altered the world.

"Yessss," he exhaled, pressing himself to me.

His scent, strong and spicy, descended over me. Huge arms encircled me in a vise. His hot breath hit my skin as he buried his face in the side of my neck, his beard tickling me.

"Um, Colonel..." I pressed my hands into his chest. My fingers sank into his long fur, pushing against the hard muscles underneath.

"Call me Grevar," he rasped, his hands roaming over my body. "Fuck. You feel so good..." He kissed my neck and palmed my breast through the thin material of the scandalous garment.

"Please..." I arched my back, leaning all the way to the mirror behind me, to get away from his insolent hands and his brazen mouth. "What are you doing?"

"I'm bedding my wife..." He rocked his hips against me, grinding his frighteningly huge erection against my lower belly.

"No." I flexed my arms, shoving at his chest in a futile attempt to get him off me.

He didn't move an inch, his chest a wide wall of muscle and fur against my efforts. At least a foot taller than me and infinitely stronger, the Colonel was about to have his way with me, and I could do nothing to stop him.

Dread slithered down my spine, chilling my insides.

"What's the worst that can happen?" I'd asked myself when agreeing to come here tonight.

It appeared I was about to find out the answer.

Somehow freeing my arms from his embrace, I grabbed his horns and yanked his head back.

"Stop it," I said loud and clear, staring straight into his eyes. Ruby-red with vertical slits for black pupils in the middle, they looked scarier than ever. "The only way you can have me tonight, Colonel, is if you *force* yourself on me."

It seemed to take a moment for my words to register with him. Eventually, the blazing storm in his eyes quieted down, and focus returned to his unhinged expression.

"Why *force*?" he asked, confusion spreading on his face. "Are you saying you don't want it?"

"No."

"Then why..." He glanced down my body.

My face heated when his eyes paused on my nipples. I felt them harden under his gaze until they poked shamelessly against the barely-there material of the nightgown. Hot tingles spread down my skin where his fur had brushed it, and my inner muscles unexpectedly clenched with need.

The sudden reaction of my body to him was extremely inconvenient. I leaned harder on the dresser for support, as my knees buckled.

"I was just trying this on," I explained, shaking my head. "I had no intentions to..."

A dark shadow moved over his face as he came closer, hovering over me.

"You are *my* wife. There can never be another man," he growled.

"There isn't..." I blinked, lost for words.

What "man" was he talking about? Why?

"Ever!" he shouted, punching his fist into the mirror behind me.

It shattered, shards raining from the dresser to the floor.

I cried out in shock. And he stepped away from me, finally allowing me to draw in some air not saturated with his scent and his heat.

He slid his stare from my face down the entire length of my body. His gaze felt smooth and hot against my skin, like the lick of a tongue. I exhaled a shuddering breath, immediately realizing that it made my breasts heave in some probably enticing fashion. I quickly crossed both arms over my chest.

"You're a young, hot-blooded woman," he gritted through his teeth, staring straight into my eyes, now. "Sooner or later you will *want* a man to fuck you. Then you'll beg me for it."

He spun on his hooves and headed for the door.

"And it can only be *me*!" he roared over his shoulder, slamming his fist against the door on his way out.

Then, I was left alone, hot and trembling.

Chapter 5

I ALLOWED AWARENESS to return fully before opening my eyes the next morning. I lay in the huge, comfy bed in the middle of the fairy-tale bedroom. The bright morning sun flooded the entire room, leaving me in lacy shade from the flowery canopy.

"Such a beautiful place," I mumbled, stretching to shake the remnants of sleep off. "Too bad it belongs to such a..." I searched my brain for a word that would best describe the Colonel. My gaze fell on my purse with the Christmas ornament. It'd been left on the night table by Omni last night. "Krampus!" I found the perfect word for that man. "He is a freaking embodiment of Krampus. And it's not just his looks."

It was a good thing Omni hadn't put the purse on the dresser last night or it would've been destroyed along with the mirror. I grabbed the purse and opened it to make sure the ornament had survived.

The familiar golden designs on the delicate, red-glass sphere glistened in the sunlight. The sight of them brought so many happy memories of our family celebrations. Lately, they always came with a hint of sadness since Grandma was gone. Christmas wasn't the same without her.

Grandma was the one who had told me about Krampus long ago. She hadn't been trying to scare me. She told me the Krampus story as a part of all the different ways that Christmas had been celebrated by people around the world.

Never, in a million years would I have thought I'd get a chance to spend Christmas with a typical Krampus one year. It was still over two months before Christmas, however, and there was no way I could stay here another night after what had happened.

I didn't feel safe in this house. After the Colonel had barged into my room last night, I could hardly sleep. I was too flustered and agitated to even cry myself to sleep. The look on his face as he lunged for me from the door still sent a rush of goosebumps down my arms.

I glanced at the side table I'd moved in front of the doors last night. Barricading them didn't do much since they were sliding doors, but it had calmed me down enough for the sleep to finally claim me. The night table was still there, as was the dresser next to it, littered with mirror shards.

"Omni..." I called hesitantly, afraid to make any sound that might send the Colonel my way again.

The frame on a stick rolled out of the closet.

"Good morning, Madam Kyradus."

I winced at *his* name again. That had to be fixed as soon as possible.

The doors slid open, and I leaped up in bed. Grabbing the bed sheet, I quickly covered myself up to my chin, even though I'd slept in my own nightshirt not that diaphanous excuse for a cloth.

To my relief, instead of the Colonel, a chubby drone flew in. It then started promptly cleaning up the shards of glass from the dresser and around it.

"I'm sorry for the mess." I felt the need to apologize, though it was hardly my fault the mirror was broken.

"This is nothing to worry about," Omni assured me in a cheerful voice. "Your breakfast," he announced as another drone, with a tray on top of it flew in.

Breakfast in bed was a great idea. The later I had to face the Colonel, the better.

"Where is...he?" I asked.

"I assume you mean the Colonel Kyradus, Madam?"

I nodded, taking a cup of warm, bitter-sweet tea from the tray that had been placed in my lap. I had hardly eaten anything for dinner. The ravenous hunger had returned at the sight of the food on the tray, and

I quickly stuffed my face with the small, round pastries that tasted like sweetened packs of clay.

"The Colonel Kyradus has left for work already," Omni informed me. "He wakes up at six. His work hours start at eight."

"Oh, he is gone. Good." Tension drained out of me at the news, my shoulders dropped with relief. I picked up a piece of fruit from the tray, it was the same size and shape as the pastries but purple in color with blue and pink swirls through it. "Did he, um, say anything?" I bit into the fruit, the thick sweet-and-sour juice coating my tongue.

"Yes, the Colonel said you're free to explore the house as you please. He will see you at dinner."

I wasn't looking forward to seeing him at all. But dinner still seemed far away. I had a whole day to myself, enough time to figure out what to do about this situation that I'd found myself in.

First, I had to call Nancy from the Liaison Committee. I couldn't wait a week until my scheduled meeting while staying here, in his house where apparently no room was safe from a late-night invasion.

More drones flew in. A few of them moved the night stand back in its place. The others disappeared behind the latticed planter to the left of the bed. When they flew out, they were carrying hangers with gray army coats and white shirts.

"What are those?" I watched the drones on their way out of the room.

"Colonel Kyradus's clothes," Omni explained. "He left the instructions for me to move them to the spare bedroom upstairs."

"What are his clothes doing in my bedroom?"

"This is the Colonel's bedroom, too. It has always been."

I set the half-eaten fruit down on the plate.

"You showed this room to me as *mine* last night."

"As the Colonel's wife, you are to share your husband's bed. From the information we've received about Earth and your country, this is the tradition in your culture, also."

"Yes, but…"

I thought back to the Colonel coming in here last night. He'd appeared calm when he'd first entered. A moment later, he'd caught the sight of my practically naked body and…well, all hell broke loose.

If this was his bedroom, the Colonel hadn't barged in with the intention to assault me. He simply was coming to bed last night. Then, he found his new "wife" dressed in hardly anything, twirling in front of the mirror…

I rubbed my face.

To the Colonel, it must've looked like I'd been waiting for him in his bedroom. I'd even changed into something sexy, as if just for him. He didn't know that for me, sex couldn't happen without forming a true connection first.

"Oh God," I groaned.

That had been the most awkward misunderstanding. Of course, the Colonel's tendency of acting without clarifying things first didn't help, but he wasn't a predator as I'd feared he was.

"You should've told me it was his bedroom, too," I reprimanded Omni. "Where did he end up sleeping, then? In the spare bedroom?"

"Yes."

"I don't want to put him out." Setting the tray aside, I jumped out of bed. "I should be the one taking the spare bedroom."

"The Colonel's instructions were to let you keep this one."

"And his orders override mine?" I asked.

"Yes."

That didn't surprise me.

"Fine."

I moved to the closet, thinking about what to do next. I'd promised to call Nancy this morning, and I needed to tell her that all was well, for now anyway.

Now, that I no longer felt in immediate danger, I'd decided not to speak to the Committee about last night, for the time being. At least not until I'd spoken to the Colonel first.

He and I needed to have a frank discussion. I wanted him to explain his expectations of me. And I needed him to listen to what I hoped to have in a marriage. I didn't want to give up on my dream of building a happy life in Voran after less than a day spent in the house of my "potential spouse." However, I didn't know how long I should be trying to pursue this dream if the reality was so very different from that.

So far, the Colonel in person had proven to be even more terrifying than his picture, and it had more to do with his attitude than his looks.

What if getting to know him better only made it worse?

I would've liked to chat about everything with my mom or my sister, but they were far away. I could only write to them once a week, and a lot could change in seven days.

"Can I make a call?"

"Interplanetary calls to your family are only possible from the headquarters of the Liaison Committee," Omni reminded.

"Yes, I know. But I'm supposed to call someone from the Committee." Nancy was largely still a stranger to me. However, since I'd promised to call, I should at least let her know that I was doing fine. I'd told her I would be, after all. "Or did the Colonel forbid me *any* calls at all?"

"No, you can call the Committee any time you wish. Would you like me to connect you?"

"Just, wait a moment. I'll make myself decent first."

I took a few seconds to browse the collection of the dresses in my closet. With tailored bodices and flared skirts, they all were my preferred style and cut. Judging by the pictures I'd seen, all of them were done in the latest fashion of Voran. Their pretty trim, gorgeous prints, and cheerful colors made me smile. The section of floor-length evening gowns was especially glamourous.

In the end, I chose to wear one of my own dresses. The familiar feel of its cut and the red-and-white checkered fabric made me feel comfortable, which was important as I was certainly out of my element in the Colonel's house.

After the quick call with Nancy to assure her I was alive and well, I came downstairs.

My thoughts rushed to last night's dinner and to what happened afterwards. Then I remembered what Omni said about the purpose of my rich wardrobe and that I would be required to accompany the Colonel to "high-profile public events."

If what the Colonel really wanted from a wife was just a glorified escort to take to balls and galas then fucking her against a dresser afterwards, then maybe we should just talk about dissolving our contract sooner rather than later. *This* wouldn't be the life I'd hoped for or wished to have.

Sadness filled me at the thought of going back to Earth with nothing but another failure under my belt.

I wandered through his grand, beautiful home. Its cheerful and elegant atmosphere clashed with what I'd learned about its owner so far.

"What's there?" I asked Omni, pointing at the smaller staircase that led down from the main floor.

"On the lower level, the Colonel Kyradus has his exercise room."

"Does it take up the entire floor?"

"Most of it. There are also bathrooms and changing areas."

I quickly ran downstairs, just to see it for myself. Instead of the gym I'd expected to find, the lower floor was a large, empty space. It had lovely wooden floors, the ceiling of average height, and walls made entirely of glass. The bright sunshine flooded a good half of the room.

"How does he exercise in here?" I asked Omni. His frame remained upstairs, but one of his drones flew down with me. "There's no equipment."

"The Colonel prefers sparring," Omni's voice came through the drone.

"With whom?"

"A number of my units have combat programs. Stay on the stairs, please. I'll show you."

The floor suddenly broke into large rectangles. Flipping over to their other side, they instantly turned the entire floor into a gym mat made of padded, dark purple leather.

"That's neat." I clicked my tongue in appreciation.

A whirring sound came from behind the stairs, then two weirdly shaped robots rolled into view. One appeared closer to a humanoid, with a pair of horns on its head, another looked very much like a large bean bag.

"They can fight each other," Omni said.

The next moment, the bean bag rolled to the horned one. Thin wires sprang out of the bean bag, forcing the humanoid robot to block their lashing.

"Or they could serve as sparring partners to someone else."

"Like the Colonel?" I watched the two robots go at each other. Their punches packed some real power and their aim was impeccable. Personally, I wouldn't want to fight one of them. They might have different settings, but I doubted the Colonel trained with them in "gentle mode," even if there was one.

Out of the entire house, this room suited the owner's personality the best—masculine and minimalistic, with a sense of barely concealed danger.

The brutal kind of energy that the Colonel radiated scared me. Even if there was no need for me to barricade my door from him every night, I felt unsettled and flustered just thinking about being in his company.

"There can never be another man."

I scoffed at his words from the previous night.

Who did he think I was that I needed that type of warning? Like I'd get so horny, I'd run searching for a random guy, one day?

"Then you'll beg me for it."

Really? Obviously, I could control my urges much better than he could.

The memory of the storm of lust in his otherworldly eyes rushed over me. The skin on my arms puckered with goosebumps again, only I wasn't sure whether those were from fear or from...something else, this time.

I rubbed my bare arms, chasing away the phantom sensation of the soft caress of his fur against my naked skin.

"We shall go back." I turned up the stairs.

When I wandered into the Colonel's spacious kitchen, an itching desire to use it took over.

My Grandma had taught me to "look for pink when things were blue." She believed there was always a spark of sunny pink in any situation, no matter how grim. Just because my hopes and dreams didn't come true on Neron, it didn't mean I couldn't enjoy at least some of what the City of Voran had to offer.

"Can I go to a store or a market, to buy a few things?" I asked Omni, sliding my hand along a glass counter top on one side of the kitchen.

"No. The Colonel did not allow for travel outside of his dwelling for you."

"Of course he didn't..." I huffed, forcing a spark of irritation down. "Well, then maybe you could help me get the ingredients? I'd love to bake something."

"Bake? I have access to over a thousand recipes. If you tell me what you want, I'll make it for you in minutes."

"Oh, but what's the fun in that?" I waved him off, moving to the mint-green, round stove in the middle of the kitchen. Two segments of glass countertop flanked it on both sides. "I'd love to make something myself."

"All right. How would you like me to assist you?"

"Can you teach me how this works?" I pointed at the stove with what appeared to be a large oven compartment underneath. "But before that, we'll need to go through whatever the Colonel has in his pantry and figure out what I can use for the ingredients."

"What are you planning to make?"

"Cupcakes." I raised my chin with a smile. "With pink frosting."

Chapter 6

FINDING THE RIGHT INGREDIENTS for my cupcakes hadn't proven easy. Omni and I started the process before lunch. It was late afternoon already, and we were still sorting through the contents of the Colonel's pantry, which occupied a spacious room just off the kitchen.

I had rows upon rows of cups filled with different powders lined up on the kitchen counter. My notebook in my lap, I was perched on a barstool, writing down English ingredients with the corresponding Voranian substitutes.

The huge bronze-colored metal sink was filled with dirty dishes from my experiments to determine the qualities and the necessary quantities of each powder. Omni's frame was hovering nearby, displaying pictures and Voranian names of the different flours and spices.

"Well, I think I could try again, using this one here as the rising agent and this one instead of vanilla..." I mumbled to myself, making notes in my book.

Absorbed in my work, I didn't hear the sound of the hooves hitting the tiled floor of the main room right away. When it registered, alarm spiked through my chest.

"The Colonel is home?" I jumped off my seat by the counter.

I knew I needed to talk to him. At the same time, I desperately wanted to avoid facing him.

The sky beyond the dome above us had changed into sunset colors already. Omni must have increased the lighting in the kitchen gradually without me noticing that the day had been slipping by. I had lost track of time and felt flustered and unprepared for the upcoming conversation.

Maybe, the Colonel would just go straight to the dining room, like he did last night? Then I could sneak upstairs quietly and pretend I went to bed early?

No such luck.

"What is all this?" The Colonel suddenly stood in the entrance of the kitchen, surveying the mess I'd made of his property.

"I—I was just trying to make some cupcakes," I replied sheepishly, realizing I'd spent the entire day on something that would normally take me an hour or less, and I had not a single cupcake to show for it. Not to mention that no one had asked me to bake anything in the first place. "I'm sorry. I'll clean it up right away…"

"Omni can clean it," the Colonel waved me off.

A couple of drones whizzed over to the sink. The water turned on as if on its own, and the drones started scrubbing the dishes.

I remained motionless, unsure of what to do with myself.

He stared at me with his unsettling eyes. I quickly swiped at my cheek, wondering if I had flour all over my face.

"Last night…" He rubbed the back of his neck, shifting his eyes from mine.

"It's fine," I took a step to the side, trying to figure out the best route to escape. "No need to apologize."

"Apologize?" He stared at me in confusion.

"Dammit," I cursed softly. "I guess you weren't going to do that anyway." I should've expected that. "Never mind. If you'll excuse me…" I inched to the door, aiming to squeeze past him.

"Daisy." He grabbed my arm, stopping me in my tracks. "Where are you going?"

"To bed?" I stilled under his stare.

"It's dinner time."

"I'm, um, not really hungry tonight."

The warmth of his large hand on my bare upper arm felt oddly pleasant, even as his grip was rather firm.

"I'm sorry to have put you out of your bedroom." I said the next thing that came into my head. "I would be more than happy to move to the spare room myself, for the remainder of my stay."

"Remainder?" he growled, his voice rolling in a deep ominous rumble. "Are you planning to leave?"

"Well, it may be too soon," I mumbled. "And I'm willing to discuss it, but considering how the things have been going... Anyway, I believe you may be willing to consider the dissolution of the contract—"

"Bullshit!" he roared, yanking me to him.

Startled, I went numb and mute at once.

"You are my wife, whether you like it or not!" he raged, holding me by my upper arms in front of him. I froze like a rabbit staring into the eyes of a snake—the blazing red eyes with pupils that looked like vertical slits left by a steel blade. "There is no leaving for you now. I won't have it!"

His unhinged anger was terrifying. I could barely blink, even my breathing all but stopped.

Then, a wave of hot defiance swelled inside me. I was so sick and tired of being scared of this man.

I drew in a deep breath, trying not to waver under his glower.

"There is no need to yell at me," I said as firmly as I could manage. I realized I was lunging into a fight against an opponent who'd won a lot of battles in his life, but this was a fight I couldn't afford to lose. "The Marriage Contract states that our union can be dissolved by either party at the end of the year. I'm considering petitioning the Committee to allow for an earlier dissolution—"

"*Both* parties." He narrowed his eyes. His jaw muscles moved, stirring his beard.

"I beg your pardon?"

"The contract can only be ended by *both* parties. And there is no way in hell I'll ever allow my wife to dishonor me by leaving like that."

Both parties.

The image of the contract rose in my mind. The words of the exit clause I'd read very carefully had been burnt into my memory. It did state "both parties." I'd just never thought that it meant "together" or "simultaneously."

Dread seized my heart. Gripped in his large hands like prey, I no longer believed any reasonable conversation was possible with this man.

Still, I tried, "Surely, you can see, this is not working between us..."

"Not without at least some effort on your part to make it work," he gritted through his teeth.

Was he accusing *me*? I couldn't believe my ears.

"*My* effort?" I gaped at him, flabbergasted. "Are you blaming *me* for all of this? You've been nothing but rough and boorish here and..." I waved my hand in the direction of the stairs, "and in the bedroom." I pointed with my gaze at his hands gripping my forearms. "*This* is no way to treat a woman."

Following my gaze, he released me, and I rubbed the lingering ache from my arms with my hands, taking a step back and away from him.

He remained in the doorway, blocking my way. Anger seethed inside me, shoving fear aside.

"Colonel—"

"Grevar," he corrected gruffly. "It's customary for the wife to address her husband by his first name."

"Gre..." I huffed a breath. "I can't. I don't think of myself as your wife. There has been no getting to know each other, no courtship, no attraction...Nothing that has to happen before the actual marriage can take place."

"You knew what you signed."

He was so right, and I felt so stupid for being naïve in my hope for an out-of-this-world romance with an alien man I'd never met, for signing my life over to him.

"When I signed, I genuinely hoped there would eventually be a connection between us." I felt deflated and crushed by disappointment all over again. "I believed you would take your time to get to know me. That you'd give me a chance to learn more about you, too. Instead, all you really wanted was...sex?"

I glared at him, feeling the anger rise higher.

His face distorted with rage. "I'm your husband! It's my right and obligation to sexually pleasure my wife. You, Madam Colonel Kyradus—"

My nerves had been stretched tight like strings. Hearing that name made me snap.

"It's *Daisy*. Like the 'flower!'" I raised my voice. "Not *Madam Kyradus*, like 'the wife of a rough, boorish Krampus.' Marriage does not give you the right to own me or to force yourself on me."

"I didn't force!" he shouted back. "I don't force myself on women. Never have. The one I've been with liked me just the way I am, 'rough and boorish.' *Especially*, in the bedroom!"

His roaring voice reverberated through the open space, amplifying under the glass dome like inside a giant bell.

"Why are you not with her, then?" I placed my fists on my hips.

His beard moved as he flexed his jaw. "She chose to be with someone else."

"Why does that not surprise me?" I shook my head.

"Enough!"

His nostrils flared as he stomped closer. Storm raged in his eyes, making me draw my head into my shoulders. I half-expected him to strike me. There'd be no way back from that.

He just stood over me, panting hard in rage.

Avoiding his terrifying eyes, I stared at one of the shiny buttons on his army coat.

"Don't you see? We're making each other miserable. Just let the Committee dissolve the contract, please, and I'll be out of here. You'll have your life back."

"No!" The word shot out of his mouth like a bullet, startling me. "You're my reward from the Governor. Refusing you would dishonor me."

"Those are the worst excuses I've ever heard for holding on to a marriage that wasn't meant to be. You can't keep me here because of some obligation toward a government official."

"I can, and I will." He stood his ground, stubborn as a goat. "Unlike you, I keep my promises and appreciate the rewards bestowed on me. I have honor."

"And I don't?" I screeched, my voice high from indignation. "How would you even know what I have? What *do* you know about me beside the fact that I own a bright sunflower dress? Nothing! Because all you care about in a wife is the convenience of having someone to fuck after dinner."

Anger boiled hot and high in my chest. The room suddenly seemed too small for both of us. This entire planet didn't have enough space for the two of us. Yet he kept standing in the doorway, blocking my way out.

"Let me go!" I snapped, shoving both hands against his shoulder with all force I could muster.

He staggered aside in shock, and I finally dashed out of the kitchen.

"Oh, I wish I'd gotten the chance to watch that video of you before I'd left Earth," I muttered under my breath while running to the stairs. "I would've never come here at all. You're nothing but a savage, in the video *and* in real life."

"You're not leaving!" he yelled after me as I ran up the main staircase that circled the entire dome. "I won't let you!"

"We'll see about that!" I screamed back.

"I said no!" he shouted. Then came the sound of the dishes crashing to the floor.

Through a section of the glass dome below, I caught a glimpse of the Colonel sweeping my neatly lined-up cups with the pre-measured ingredients off the counter. The shards of glass scattered all over the floor, clouds of powder rising through the air.

"Savage." I gritted my teeth, seething with anger. Rushing into the bedroom, I slid the doors shut behind me. "A wild animal. A raging beast. The freaking Krampus..."

I paced the room, trying to calm my nerves and my breathing.

There was absolutely no way I was staying under the same roof with this man for an entire year, not to mention for the rest of my life. I needed to get out of here as soon as possible.

"Omni, get Nancy, the human representative to the Liaison Committee on the line, please."

The robot rolled out from the closet. "Unfortunately, I cannot comply with your request. The Colonel had just cancelled his permission for any outgoing calls for you, Madam Kyradus."

The last shreds of my composure evaporated at the sound of that name again.

"*Daisy*! It's *Daisy*!" I screamed. "There is no *Madam Kyradus*. You hear me? He doesn't deserve to have a wife because he has no idea how to be a good husband. Breaking things, raging like a wild beast, and depriving me of all contact with the outside world is the *opposite* of what a good husband would do."

Tears sprang to my eyes, spurred by the feeling of utter helplessness. Here, in his house, I was entirely at his mercy. He could lock me up, starve me, hide me from the world if he felt so inclined. I couldn't leave unless he allowed it. I couldn't even sneak out, because I had no idea how to operate the freaking aircraft.

Taking deep breaths, I stopped pacing eventually and tried to think rationally.

No, he *couldn't* hide me from the world.

As the first human-Voranian couple, the Colonel and I were watched by the entire populations of two planets.

My first follow-up meeting with the Committee was in a few days. There would be major consequences if I failed to show up for it. The meetings were scheduled weekly for the next month while the human delegation remained in Voran. After the humans left for Earth, the meetings were supposed to happen monthly.

Either way, I would get plenty of opportunities to plead my case for dissolution of this joke of a marriage. Meanwhile, I should gather the evidence of the Colonel's abusive behaviour to prove my case.

Having a plan—however shaky—made me feel a little better. I was not alone, the people of two planets were watching the progress of this marriage. If I did get locked up, everyone would know.

With the adrenaline still rushing through my system, I knew I wouldn't be able to fall asleep quickly tonight. I felt too agitated, angry, and...overwhelmingly sad. Even if a romantic relationship between us wasn't meant to be, I'd still hoped for a friendship between the Colonel and I, or at least for some kind of understanding.

I hadn't expected this to end this badly.

"Could you draw me a bath, please?" I asked Omni, heading to the closet to get rid of my dress.

"Certainly," the robot replied, rolling with me to the closet and from there to the adjacent bathroom.

Preoccupied with my gloomy thoughts, I began undressing in the robot's presence. It was just a machine, after all.

The clear, round tub stood in the middle of the bathroom. A blown glass chandelier hung over it, dripping with vines and flowers. The tub had no faucet. The water simply rose from the bottom, filling the entire tub within seconds. A pleasant fragrance drifted through the room with the steam.

"Oh, it looks fantastic. Thank you, Omni." After taking off my bra and underwear, I raised a leg over the edge of the tub to climb in when Omni's screen lit up brightly.

"Colonel Kyradus is on the line for you," Omni informed me.

The Colonel's grumpy face suddenly filled the screen.

"I don't want to talk to him." I climbed into the tub and stood inside it, waiting for my feet to adjust to the temperature of the water. Omni had made it just a bit too hot.

The Colonel's jaw dropped, he blinked, staring straight at me. I realized belatedly that he must be able to see me, as well.

"Oh no!" I hugged my bare breasts with both arms and plopped into the tub with a huge splash. "Stop showing me to him! I said I don't want to talk to him."

Thankfully, Omni's screen immediately went black.

"The Colonel expressed concern that you're hungry," Omni stated calmly. "He is requesting your presence at dinner."

Concern, requesting. I doubted the Colonel had used these actual words. Most likely, he'd yelled, stomped his hooves, and broke a few more things. That seemed to be his only way of "expressing" himself. I didn't think he even had any nice words in his vocabulary, which was filled mostly with growls and grunts.

"I'm not hungry," I replied sulkily, sinking into the fragrant water up to my chin. "Tell him to have dinner without me."

"Would you allow the Colonel to send some food up here for you?"

Would I allow?

Was he actually asking for my permission? Now?

It was probably just Omni's program, dressing up the Colonel's "requests" into more socially appropriate form.

"No. He can eat it all himself."

I sank even deeper into the water, until it touched my lips. The warmth finally started to relax me a little.

A few minutes later, Omni's voice came up again, "Colonel Kyradus would like to know if you would at least have the dessert."

Dessert? I didn't get any last night, either.

"What's for dessert?" I asked, tentatively.

"*Phesoth* mousse with *chesu* berries and whipped *aicea*. It's a delicacy in Voran."

Maybe I was just a little bit hungry, after all.

"Fine. He can send it by drone," I conceded.

It hadn't escaped me that the Colonel was doing the entire negotiation in his own name. He could've just sent the food up here through Omni, without saying it was from him.

"Thanks," I said, accepting a small crystal dish from a drone. If Omni felt like forwarding my thanks to the Colonel, it was his business.

Soaking in the luxurious bath, the crystal dish with something heavenly delicious in my hand, I finally was able to completely relax for the time being.

That was my spark of sunny pink in this utterly blue situation.

Chapter 7

"COLONEL KYRADUS IS requesting a meeting with you." Omni's voice woke me up.

The sky above glowed faintly with the sunrise. The bed's canopy also lit up slowly, aiding the pale light from the outside in illuminating the bedroom.

"A meeting?" I sat up, rubbing the sleep out of my eyes.

For the past two days, the Colonel and I had been effectively avoiding each other. It hadn't been difficult as he left for work before I woke. He also ate the dinner elsewhere, coming home only after I had gone to bed.

"Why?" I asked Omni. "What time is it?"

"Six thirty," came the deep voice of the Colonel from the door.

I jumped up at the sound of his voice. Any remnants of sleep now gone, I yanked the covers up to my chin.

"I'll be leaving for work shortly." Fully dressed in his uniform, his horns polished to a shine, and his fur smoothed down, he appeared collected and refreshed—more civilized than I had ever seen him. "I need to talk to you before I go."

"What is it?" I shifted under the covers uneasily.

"The Governor's Ball is tonight. I have been invited to attend. The Governor is requesting I bring my new wife along."

"Me?"

"Evidently." He tilted his head, folding his arms over his chest.

"I—I don't think that's a good idea." Not when I was determined to leave here at the first opportunity. Going out in public as Colonel's wife would only perpetuate the lie that ours was a valid marriage.

His chest rose with a deep breath, his eyes focused on mine.

"Please," he said suddenly.

I nearly choked on the air I inhaled. I hadn't heard the word "please" from him before. I didn't think he even knew it existed.

"Why?" I glanced at him suspiciously, searching for signs of hidden motives in his expression.

I'd figured that the purpose of him getting a wife in the first place was so that she would escort him to some high-profile events. The Governor's Ball must be an important one to attend, since he'd actually asked me nicely. He wasn't shouting or breaking things. Not yet, anyway.

"This marriage was the Governor's idea—" he started.

"Oh, I get it. You want to show him that you appreciate his gift? And with the *gift* being me, I'll need to play along. Right?"

He took his time to reply, his jaw moving under his beard, eyes set on me. "Right."

I couldn't immediately decide whether his straightforwardness was insulting or admirable, but I was determined to be honest in return.

"Well, you see, doing that wouldn't be helping my intentions. Because I believe it's best to dissolve this marriage."

The muscles in his face twitched. He balled his hands into fists. Surprisingly, no explosion followed. Having witnessed his temper, I appreciated his current composure.

"Why?" he asked in a rough, low voice.

"Why?" I repeated in shock. "Are you kidding me? Do you really not see the problem here?" I waved my hand between us. "You've done nothing but yell and growl at me ever since I got here. And I don't particularly enjoy the idea of being yelled and growled at for the rest of my life."

He shifted hoof to hoof.

"You have yelled, too."

My own temper heated at this accusation.

"Because you yelled first!"

"You're yelling at me, right now," he observed, infuriatingly calmly.

"Fuck," I cursed under my breath. Hiding my face in my hands, I inhaled deeply, willing my agitation to subside.

Normally, it would take a lot to set me off. The Colonel had managed to do it within seconds of his arrival.

"I would also like you to reconsider exposing our domestic situation to the Committee this week." His voice sounded strained, the calm in it forced. "I don't want any government organizations to stick their noses into my private life. What happens in my household is entirely *my* business."

"Not *entirely*," I objected. "Not when I'm a part of your household too. For now, anyway."

"Daisy." He heaved a breath, moving my way.

I scooted all the way to the opposite end of the mattress as he came closer and sat on the edge of the bed.

"Only a fraction of males in Voran ever have the opportunity to get married," he said. "Mine was presented to me at a state-wide ceremony, with our high officials and a large part of the city's population present. I was not the only one who waited for your arrival on our planet. If our marriage works, many more Voranian men would get a chance to have a human wife."

"But it's *not* working..." I shook my head slowly.

"Maybe," he agreed. "But if my highly anticipated wife takes off mere days after her arrival, it'd cause a highly-publicized scandal that I may never fully recover from."

"A scandal?"

Was *that* what he really worried about? His reputation?

"So, you're concerned about what strangers may think of you?" I squinted at him. "You want to present yourself in the best light possible to the city, but you don't care at all about your behavior at home?"

He winced.

"I don't care what strangers think about me, but I am concerned about the future of this program."

"Are you now?" That the Colonel cared about anything at all was news to me. "Then why didn't you tell me that before? Why have you not made any attempt at a courteous conversation with me until now?"

"I, er...conversed," he objected.

I shook my head and rolled my eyes in exasperation.

"What we had weren't conversations. Even before the yelling started, there'd been just grunts, single-word answers, and strained arguments."

Did he really believe those were all parts of a loving relationship between a husband and wife?

"I saw—" He stopped then corrected himself, "I *see* no reason to act as someone different than who I am. With anyone, not just with my wife."

"So, you're saying that's who you are? You're *always* the miserable fuck you've been for the past four days?"

He made a face.

"For a woman, you sure swear a lot."

"And as a typical man, you bring that out in me," I retorted.

He lifted one thick eyebrow, but didn't say anything.

I was really impressed by his self-control this morning. So, he *could* hold his anger back when he really wanted to, even though he looked rather stiff and uncomfortable. It must've cost him a huge effort to control that explosive temper of his.

I did my best to remain relatively calm, too. A little too late maybe, but we finally were having a real conversation here.

"I need to warn you," I said. "I'm not particularly good at socializing with governors. I've never met one before. I'd have no idea what to say or what to do."

"You won't have to do anything, just be yourself." He shrugged.

"Be myself?" I snorted a laugh. "Be careful what you ask for, Colonel."

His expression had smoothed out somewhat.

"Even if you end up doing something out of the norm, no one would hold it against you. You've come from another planet. Some oddity in your behavior would be understandable and even expected."

Thinking of myself as an "oddity" made me smile.

"And you think you'll be okay showing up in public with the 'odd' alien woman? People will be staring at us, I'm sure."

"Oh, they will." His beard suddenly parted with a smile, too. It was small, barely there, but it broke through nevertheless. "Let them stare. If anyone dares to do more than that, they'd have to deal with me. You'll have nothing to worry about."

The easy confidence with which he'd taken on the task of protecting me from the crowd was appealing.

I drew in some air. The morning seemed brighter now as if a storm had dissipated. I decided to use the moment before it was gone.

"If I do what you're asking from me, would you let me go?" I wasn't fooling myself. The Colonel had decided to be reasonable this one morning just because he needed something from me. I had to use this opportunity to clarify a few things.

Just like that, the smile disappeared off his face, his expression shut down.

"You can't leave."

I dug in my heels. "But I can't stay. If you keep insisting, you'd be holding me here against my will. The Committee—"

He groaned, raking his fingers through the fur on his head.

"Leave the Committee out of it." Leaping off the bed, he paced in front of me. "Do you really hate it here so much?" He stopped abruptly, facing me.

I crumpled the sheet in my hands, clutching it to my chest. It wasn't the place I hated. My decision to leave had everything to do with him, not his house or this planet.

"I can't see myself spending the rest of my life here, with you," I said, being brutally honest. "We are too..."

Similar, it dawned on me.

I'd wanted to say that we were too different, but I suddenly realized that the opposite might be true. We were too similar to get along. We both had a temper. Except that I'd never even realized I had one until now. The Colonel had brought it out in me. He proved to be capable of getting my blood to boil with a word or even a glare. In addition, both of us had the tendency to act or say things first and think later.

"If you leave within days after your arrival," the Colonel explained. "I would become the subject of public resentment and most likely a government investigation. Despite being a public figure, I am a private person, Daisy. I'd like to avoid the scrutiny and intrusion into my home and my personal life."

"You understand that is not enough for me to stay married to you?"

"Possibly," he tipped his horns in a nod. "But would you reconsider leaving immediately?"

I mulled over his request for a moment. When asked nicely, I'd always had a hard time saying no.

"Is it that important to you?"

"Yes," he replied, his expression open and sincere.

I heaved a sigh.

"Why wouldn't you talk to me like this before? Why yell and toss things?"

He slid his gaze aside, looking if not exactly ashamed then at least somewhat remorseful.

"Hard day at work and inherently bad temper," he confessed then admitted, "the lack of full understanding of the situation, too."

I huffed a short laugh. "Well, I've always found honesty an admirable quality in people."

"Will you stay, then?"

"Will you sign the dissolution of the marriage contract?"

He paused, his mouth pressed into a stubborn line.

I folded my arms across my chest. "That *is* the deal. Your reputation and the future of the liaison program in exchange for my freedom."

"How long are you willing to stay with me?" he asked in turn.

I still felt uneasy in his presence. However, this conversation gave me hope. The immediate future no longer seemed that scary or bleak.

"I suppose I could stay until the end of the month when the ship of our delegation is scheduled to depart." There were no other ships leaving for Earth until then, anyway.

"That's too soon," he shook his head energetically. "The contract stipulates at least a year."

"It depends on how things go." I stood my ground. "Daily shouting matches may make even a month seem too long. A year of that may drive me to jumping off one of your glass domes rather than staying a moment longer under the same roof with you."

"Don't jump." His frown deepened as he sat on the bed again, this time on my side of the mattress.

"I'd prefer not to." I drew my legs up under the covers, to make more room for him. "Let's just try to talk first, yell second. You and me, both. Okay?"

He tipped his horns with brief nod.

"Will you come to the Ball tonight, then?"

I heaved a breath. "Is it important for you that I come?"

"Yes. The Governor is not just the head of our country, he is also a very good friend of mine. I'd love to honor his request."

"Well. Since that's kind of a part of the deal we've just made, I'll come."

"Thank you." He got up from the bed.

Smoothing the fur over his temples with his hands, he then adjusted his uniform and said in a rather formal tone, "I'll pick you up right after work. Be ready."

I THOUGHT ABOUT THE Governor's Ball all morning. Now, that I'd agreed to go, I wanted to do it right. After breakfast, I asked Omni to show me some pictures of past Governor's Ball events.

Apparently, the head of the Voranian government loved to party. There were not one, but three balls at his palace, in the last year alone. The one the Colonel and I were going to tonight seemed to have no other purpose but to honor the Colonel and to display his new human wife to Voranian society.

I understood now why the Colonel had made an effort to ensure my appearance there. He couldn't possibly show up to the gathering of people who had come specifically to gawk at an alien from another planet without said alien on his arm.

That meant I'd be the center of attention, no matter what I did or wore. However, if everyone was about to gawk at me, I wanted them to at least do it for all the right reasons.

I studied the dresses of the few women in attendance at the previous events, then went to my closet in search of something similar but even better. I wanted to make myself look amazing for the occasion. After all, I was coming to the event as the wife of the man in charge of the entire Voranian Army, and I'd agreed to play the part.

Thankfully, my well-stocked closet offered plenty of suitable options. After trying on a number of stunning gowns, I finally decided to go with one in blush chiffon with pink-gold embroidery on the bodice, cup-sleeves, and a flowing multi-layered skirt. Its style was elegant enough for such a high-profile occasion as the Governor's Ball promised to be, yet also sweet and breezy to appeal to my personal tastes.

Close to dinner time, I changed into the dress and did my make-up. Omni managed to curl my hair for me, after I had explained to him exactly how it had to be done. I even had a suitable barrette in rose gold encrusted with tiny crystals and pearls. And I found a pair of gorgeous, crystal-studded sandals on one of the shoe shelves in the closet.

By the time Omni informed me of the landing of the Colonel's aircraft, I was completely dressed and ready to go.

With one last quick look in the brand-new mirror that had replaced the broken one, I rushed out of the room.

A light flutter of anticipation lifted my spirits. A party always meant fun, didn't it?

This could be an exciting night after all.

GREVAR

"Welcome home, Colonel Kyr—"

"Where is she?" he cut the AI off.

Since Daisy had taken up the residence in his house, coming home didn't feel the same. A female presence under his roof in general had been foreign to him. He'd even programed his AI as male. Having an actual woman living here was an entirely new experience.

Before her, coming home meant time to relax, unwind, and even be lazy for a while. Now, everything inside him heated up and buzzed with excitement the moment he crossed the threshold.

Although Daisy seemed to be keeping mostly to the bedroom, even in his absence, she left traces of her presence throughout his space—from re-arranging the hanging plants on the breakfast patio to allow for more sunlight in the area where she must be taking her tea late in the morning, to having a lot of still-shots of the life in Voran saved in Omni's memory.

Even the smell of the baking ingredients in the pantry now reminded him of her.

And the feeling didn't end the moment he left for work in the morning. His thoughts tended to drift to her throughout the day.

He found office work irritating, and often more challenging than even facing an attack of *fescods* on a battlefield. Overall, working from an office, of course, was safer than fighting on the frontlines on Tragul, the planet where *fescods* still remained active. He had taken the safety of the office into consideration when accepting the promotion. He had a family, and his sons needed him well and alive.

Living in the city also allowed him to remain close to his children's school. He liked being just a short flight away from them, at all times.

"I told her to be ready." He stomped into the main room. Irritation stirred under his skin. The fucking meeting had taken longer than he'd planned. There was no time left now to wait for a woman to powder her nose for hours.

"I'm ready!" Daisy's clear, melodious voice sounded from the top of the stairs.

He blinked, letting his jaw drop, as he took in the vision of rose chiffon and bouncing curls that was his wife running down the stairs to him.

The skirt of her dress billowed around her in a voluminous wave. The embroidered bodice tightly hugged her enticing curves in all the right places. The neckline was low enough to display the delicate swells of her breasts in an extremely appealing way, yet high enough to be appropriate for the event he was taking her to.

Her gray-blue eyes twinkled with excitement. Her bright, light-orange hair framed her lovely face like sunshine.

"I'm ready." She stopped on the last step, catching her breath. "Do I look okay?"

"You are..." He let his gaze travel down her entire figure in admiration, then fought the sudden urge to reach for her. He wished to know exactly how her body would feel in his arms if he hugged her just the way she was, wrapped in the fabric of the dress. "So..." The words seemed to have deserted him.

Then, his gaze fell on her shoes. On her *toes*, actually. That was what he recalled those short appendages of humans were called. They proved to be the most bizarre thing about her, even more so than the lack of horns.

Disproportionally shorter than the fingers, the *toes* were squished together by the bejeweled straps of her sandals. The bright red color she had painted the toe nails with—identical to that on the nails on her hands—made them look even more like disfigured fingers.

Grotesque. Even creepy.

"Um..." Obviously catching his stare, she shuffled her feet back, hiding them under the hem of her long skirt. "I probably should change..."

"No." He realized belatedly he hadn't guarded his expression while staring at her feet. "Don't change a thing. You look beautiful."

He reached for her.

Shaking her head, she backed up the stairs, away from him. The spark of happy excitement faded from her eyes.

"I'll be right back." She spun on her heels, dashing back up the stairs.

"Daisy!" he called after her, hating himself. "You look stunning, I swear! *All* of you."

With a flash of pink chiffon, she disappeared behind the bedroom doors.

Chapter 8

"DAISY." THE COLONEL shifted jerkily as we both sat in the aircraft, soaring through the sunset sky.

"I'm fine. Everything is cool."

Saying it didn't make things "fine." I knew that. I just really couldn't take another argument at the moment. My capacity to cope with yelling had overflowed long ago.

Not that the Colonel looked or sounded like he was about to yell again.

"It's not *fine*." He tapped something on the control panel then turned to me.

He took my hand in his unexpectedly, sending all my thoughts in disarray.

"Don't you...you know, need to fly this thing?" I mumbled. Snatching my hand from him, I waved at the lights of the control panel.

"It's a self-flying aircraft."

"But didn't you steer it before? On our way from the spaceport to your house?" I glanced down at the tall glass structures of Voran floating by below. The aircraft didn't appear to be losing altitude or whirring off course.

"I needed something to occupy my hands with at the time."

"Why?"

"To help me deal with being..." he winced, not meeting my eye. "With being nervous."

I struggled with the idea of the Colonel ever feeling nervous, he seemed so unshakably sure of himself at all times.

"Did *I* make you feel that way?" I stared at him incredulously. "People don't usually get nervous around *me*. I've been called easy-going and down-to-earth—all those things people say about someone who makes them feel comfortable, with whom they don't have to watch what they say or do. You know, someone like a close family member—that one harmless, bubbly cousin everyone seems to have, the one who never gets offended for long and just smiles—"

He reached for my hand again, interrupting my blabbing.

"You look beautiful, Daisy. I mean it."

I shoved my feet deeper under my seat.

Back at his house, I'd changed from the open-toe sandals into a pair of white, ankle-high booties. Their wedge heels even gave my feet a hoof-like appearance.

"The dress is perfect on you," he insisted.

"Okay. Thank you." I worried my hand would start to sweat any minute now, clasped in his big, warm palm. I tugged at it, but he wouldn't let go.

"And the sandals were beautiful, too. You didn't need to change."

"No. I'm glad I did." I glanced up at him. "You see, I'm not ashamed of my toes. I've had them for over twenty-five years now, and I love them just the way they are. I've painted them in pretty colors and proudly displayed them in strappy sandals and flip-flops all my life. I'm not embarrassed by having feet, no matter what you may think about them. The only reason I've changed my shoes is because I really couldn't handle seeing the same look you had back there on the face of every Voranian I'm about to meet tonight." I heaved a long breath. "Not tonight. It's already been a very stressful few days."

I tried to take my hand away from him again, but he laced my fingers with his then covered my hand with his other hand. There was no way for me to retrieve it now, and I decided I didn't want to take it away after all, leaving it in his possession. My hand felt rather nice, cradled there in the warmth of his two large, rough palms.

"I didn't mean to offend you, Daisy." His voice was deep, his tone as gruff as always. However, a softer note slipped into it. "It just... It was unexpected."

"My scary toes?" I rolled my eyes.

"You've worn closed-toe shoes before tonight, and I've never seen bare feet before," he explained, sounding defensive. "I've heard of toes, but... I'm sorry, okay? Can you forget about all of this, please? I want you to enjoy tonight."

I thought back to meeting the Voranians for the first time, at the spaceport. Quite a few of their physical attributes had shocked me then, their hooves included. Even my sister had called the Colonel "scary-looking."

"I understand. I'm not offended," I said to him. I never could stay upset with someone for too long, anyway. "I thought your eyes were scary, too, at first."

"My eyes?" He blinked. "Scary?"

"Humans don't have red eyes. Seeing them was a bit unsettling at first."

"At first." He tilted his head to the side. "But how about now?"

I looked up, finding his eyes with mine. Sitting this close to him in the confined space of the aircraft, with my hand held in both of his, awareness suddenly rushed me, and I dropped my gaze down, saying nothing.

"I've been told I have *fierce* eyes." His voice dipped lower, an unfamiliar velvet note in it reached deep inside my chest with warm resonance. "Do you still find them scary, Daisy?"

He slid a finger under my chin, lifting my head and forcing me to meet his eyes again—fire red, with coal-black slits for pupils.

"Definitely *fierce*," I said quietly. My head was spinning slightly, as if I were falling somewhere. Maybe under a spell? I swallowed hard. "Intense, but not scary."

He leaned closer, brushing his thumb along my lower lip, and I quickly tucked it between my teeth. The aircraft seemed way too small all of a sudden, the vivid colors of the sunset closed in all around us.

"Are we there yet?" I asked, unable to tear my gaze away from his eyes that appeared to grow brighter and hotter.

"There?" As if yanked back to the reality, he blinked, his bushy eyebrows moved closer. "Yes. Almost. But there was something else I wanted to do before we arrive."

Leaning over my lap, he slid open an aircraft compartment in front of me and took out a flat, orange box.

"I want you to wear these tonight."

He opened the lid of the box and took out a cluster of orange-green balls, each about the size of a marble.

"What is it?" I squinted at them, wondering what he meant by me wearing this.

"It's the jewelry set my father gifted to my mother when he was courting her."

The baubles looked more like a child's dress-up beads than anything a grown woman would wear, but I loved the bright shimmering colors.

"It's pretty."

Shifting closer, he circled my neck with the necklace, closing the clasp at my nape. The numerous strings of baubles draped over my entire chest, nearly reaching my waist.

"Did she end up marrying him?" I felt very much like a Christmas tree now, hung with bright, round ornaments.

"She did." He took out two spirals strung with the same balls of orange, green, and brown swirls. "This is *shalel*, an extremely rare mineral mined only on the planet Aldrai. My father paid a fortune for this set, back in the day. And it's truly priceless, now." He wrapped one spiral around each of my forearms. "My father gave it to me after the ceremony at the Governor's Palace last year, right after the announcement of my upcoming marriage was made."

I'd been excited to be selected as the first bride to go to Neron. For the Colonel, I understood, this marriage held an even bigger significance. In Voran, our union was a state affair—a really big deal.

"I am the first son of my father's to get married," the Colonel continued. "He wanted you to have this."

"Thank you."

I took out my fresh-water pearl studs to let him put the long strings of baubles in my ears.

"How many brothers do you have?" I asked while he was doing it.

"Four. The fifth one died at birth, along with my mother."

"Oh, no," I gasped. "I'm so sorry, Colonel."

He furrowed his brow slightly, moving a shoulder back. "It happened more than thirty-four years ago. Enough time has passed."

"Time definitely helps." I released a sigh. "But do we ever fully heal from a loss? My Grandma passed away when I was sixteen, and I still miss her every day."

"How about the rest of your family?" he asked after a pause. "Are they well?"

"Yes. My parents are alive and well. And I have an older sister, who is married and has two children, a boy and a girl, my niece and nephew." I smiled, thinking about all of them.

He stared at me intensely.

"You miss them." It wasn't a question.

"I do." I nodded, stifling another sigh.

"Is that why you want to go back home?"

"What? No. I've made the conscious decision to leave my home and family to come here."

"Why did you come to Voran, Daisy?"

This question he should have asked me a long time ago. Preferably even before he had made the call to bring me here. He should have asked me why I was ready to move planets to come live with him. Or better yet, he should've read my damn letter.

I inhaled deeply then looked straight into those bright red eyes of his. There was no point in lying, it's not like I needed to worry about what he'd think of me, now.

"Because I hoped to find my place and my purpose here, Colonel. I was looking forward to making my home here and to raising a family with you."

"My family," he echoed.

"Right."

I had hoped that he, his children, and I might all become one happy family one day, but that seemed like another lifetime, now—the time when I still had silly hopes and before I had the "pleasure" of meeting the Colonel in person.

I turned away, and we sat in silence for a few moments.

Never a fan of silence unless I was alone, I broke it first, "Where are your brothers? And your dad?"

"They all live in Kixel, the small town where I grew up."

"Are they coming to visit you any time soon?"

"No."

He promptly lifted another string of balls from the box, leaning in to inspect my ear again.

"How many holes do you have pierced in your ear?" he asked, obviously changing the subject.

I shifted in my seat. "Just one in each."

"All right then." He dropped the remaining baubles back into the box then put the whole thing back into the compartment. "These will have to do."

HANDS SPLAYED ON THE glass of the aircraft side, I stared at the brilliant cluster of glass domes on top of a wide skyscraper. Lit from within with multi-colored lights, the entire structure stood out against the dying sunset like a humongous precious jewel.

"The Governor's Palace," the Colonel announced, gesturing at the magnificent contraption of glass, color, and light.

The aircraft pulled over and landed on a small open platform with a glass walkway connected to it. The edge of the walkway fused with the side of our aircraft, sealing out the winter air. The door of the aircraft slid open, and we both got out.

The short walkway led us under the first glass dome.

"Wow!" I spun around, taking in the shimmering lights under the tall arches of bright, luscious flower garlands everywhere.

Voranians dressed in bright clothing lingered in small groups here. Everyone's attention shifted to me as soon as I set my foot on the lush grass under the dome. But the main party appeared to be happening under the largest dome of the cluster, straight ahead.

"Let's go." The Colonel offered me his elbow in a gallant gesture.

A huff of air escaped from my chest. A hefty dose of anxiety mixed in with my excitement and anticipation.

"Okay." I gripped his arm, plastering a wide smile on my face. "Let's do this."

As we moved under the main glass dome, the attention of the crowd thickened. Curious stares glided down my body, making my skin prickle with unease and the fine hairs on my arms stand up. My heart raced as I wondered what they all thought about me—the pale, hornless, and tailless redhead from another planet.

The Voranians themselves presented something amazing to look at. The males' richly decorated clothes had been obviously created to attract attention. Most men present had their hooves and horns painted with designs that matched their outfits.

The Colonel steered me to a group of men in the middle of the room. A circle of them parted as we approached, revealing a tall male in a long dress coat in gold, green, and white. His lemon-yellow eyes lit up with excitement when his gaze fell on me.

"Oh, and there she is! You've been keeping her all to yourself for way too long, Kyradus." He took a few steps to us and grabbed my free hand in both of his. "Madam Colonel." He smiled, tipping his elaborately painted horns my way.

"Governor Ashir Kaeya Drustan," the Colonel introduced the man to me.

"Oh, Governor..." Having no clue of what the protocol was or even if there was one, I dipped into a curtsy. "I am very honored to meet you."

"Isn't she a delight?" the Governor gushed, glancing over his shoulder to his entourage as if inviting them to join in his admiration. "Polite and lovely. And so exotic." He yanked down a lock of my hair that had fallen over my shoulder, watching with clear fascination as the curl bounced back when he released it. "Just between you and me," he leaned closer, as if about to share a secret with me, "I find the rest of your human delegation exceptionally dull and boring."

I found nothing to say to that, simply smiling wider and staring at him like a complete idiot.

"Tell me, Madam Colonel, how do you find life on Neron, so far?" he asked me. His lemon eyes twinkled with curiosity from under his impossibly long eyelashes.

His lively, out-going manner put me at ease, melting some of the initial apprehension. I didn't even mind his way of talking about me as if I were an exotic bird at first.

"Well, I haven't seen much of Neron yet," I ventured carefully, hoping it didn't sound like a complaint.

"Still," he insisted, waving his hand at the room and the crowd that now surrounded us. "All of this must be so very different from what you're used to."

"Oh yes, it is." I kept my gaze on him, trying to ignore the growing number of Voranians congregating around us. The attention of the entire ballroom-full of people was overwhelming. "The differences between our worlds are mind-blowing. But to help me feel at home in Voran, I prefer to focus on similarities for now."

His groomed eyebrows shot up to his horns painted with green vines and golden flowers.

"Do you find there are many similarities?" he sounded incredulous.

"Quite a few." I nodded firmly. "Possibly even more than differences."

He tilted his head, curiosity shining through his expression.

"Pray tell."

"Well, like humans, Voranians have two eyes, two hands, a nose, and a mouth." I stopped myself from saying *two feet*.

Tossing his head back, the Governor released a loud, hearty laugh.

"Cannot argue with that!" He shook his head, turning to the crowd around us.

The men laughed in response, too, clapping their hands.

"What else?" He gazed back at me, excitement bouncing in his eyes.

"Like you, we live in houses, build cities, and travel in vehicles." I thought about the reasons why the Colonel had been rewarded with a marriage and why he'd been insisting on keeping it. "Both our species value courage, loyalty, and friendship. All of us hold honor and gratitude in high regard. That is a good start, I think."

"It most certainly is." The Governor kept smiling, looking both amused and impressed.

The man at his right lowered his head to his boss's ear. "I beg your pardon, Governor, but we're on a tight schedule, tonight."

I followed his gaze, glancing back over my shoulder. A line seemed to be gathering behind us. People waited for their turn to greet the Head of the State.

"Kyradus," the Governor addressed my husband, who remained by my side. "Make sure you bring her by again before you two leave tonight." He then turned to me, squeezing my hand in both of his once again. "I'd love to hear what you think about our little event."

Chapter 9

GAPING AT MY SURROUNDINGS, I almost forgot that everyone at the ball was gaping at me. A colorful band of Voranian men played lively music on the stage under the garlands of white and gold flowers. Shiny chrome stands with trays of finger foods and drinks glided through the crowd.

Feeling like an outsider, I was grateful to the Colonel for sticking by my side. People kept coming up to us to talk to him and to gawk at me.

"Grevar!" A high voice shrilled though the air suddenly.

An unusually short Voranian appeared in front of us. A female, I realized, spotting her pink-and-yellow dress that highlighted her bright magenta eyes.

"I'm so happy to see you." She grabbed the Colonel by his ears, yanking his head down for a smooch on his lips.

Apparently, Voranian women were even friendlier than the men, the usual two-handed handshake didn't cut it for her.

"You brought your wife?" She turned to me with a delighted smile.

"Hi—" I started, but she didn't let me finish. Getting hold of my ears, she placed an energetic kiss on my mouth, too.

Was that a Voranian women's thing, then? To kiss strangers as a form of greeting?

I could taste her sweet lipstick on my lips. From the corner of my eye, I glimpsed the Colonel discreetly wiping his mouth with the fur on the back of his hand. I couldn't do the same as my ears were still firmly gripped in the dainty fingers of the tiny woman.

"I'm so proud of Grevar," she gushed. "He got a wife!"

"Lucky man." I wiggled my eyebrows.

"Luck has nothing to do with it." She shook her head, the strings of tiny silver bells on the tips of her horns clinked melodiously with the gesture. "He totally earned it. Right, cousin?"

"Cousin?" I glanced at the Colonel.

"Lievoa," he introduced the woman to me. "One of the four children of my father's brother."

"And the only daughter," Lievoa added with pride, finally letting go of my ears that now felt flaming hot.

"I'm Daisy." I dipped my head in a polite bow.

"I know. Your name was announced as soon as Grevar had selected you." She leaned a little closer. "It must've been a difficult task. I've heard there were thousands of applications to choose from."

"Exactly," I said, not hiding the sarcasm in my voice for the benefit of the Colonel who remained in the earshot. "The selection process *should've* taken weeks, if not months."

"Apparently, it took him less than an hour!" She pressed her clasped hands to her chest. "He must've known you were *the one* the moment he saw your picture. It was destiny."

"Destiny," I muttered under my breath. "Or a bright 'lucky' dress."

A group of men approached the Colonel, diverting his attention from us.

"Speaking of dresses." Lievoa glanced down my body. "You like this one?"

"This?" I smoothed my hand down the soft, luxurious fabric. "I love it."

"Really?" She beamed at me another delighted smile. "Oh, it makes me so happy. It came from my dress shop."

"It did?"

"Surely, you didn't think that Grevar assembled the entire wardrobe for you all on his own. As soon as your sizes had been confirmed, he called me in panic, begging for help."

I slid my hand down my skirt again. Panicking and begging definitely didn't appear like the Colonel's style. However, something inside me warmed at the thought that he hadn't been completely indifferent about my arrival.

"The wardrobe is exquisite. The dresses, the shoes... I should have known he'd had some help."

"Of course he did." She threw a sympathetic look at the Colonel, who was talking to the group of men and could no longer hear us. "The poor guy has been wearing nothing but army uniforms most of his life. He had no idea where to even begin as far as women's clothing was concerned. Luckily, I have great taste. Most of the dresses I sell in my shop I design myself."

"You do? Is this one your design, as well?"

"Yes!"

I touched, the embroidery of my bodice with a new appreciation.

"This is amazing, Lievoa. You're very talented."

"Thank you." She smiled wide at me. "There aren't that many women in Voran who can truly appreciate a well-made garment."

"Well, there aren't that many women in Voran. Period." I laughed. "You are the first one I've met."

"Oh no! We need to rectify that. Come." She tugged me by my hand. "I'll introduce you to the women here that I know."

The Colonel looked up from his conversation, casting us a concerned glance, as Lievoa dragged me away.

"I'll be right back," I assured him, before following the clinking of the silver bells that adorned the horns of his cousin.

"Have you met the twins yet?" Lievoa asked me on the way.

"You mean the Colonel's children?"

She nodded, creating a series of melodious thrills from her bells.

"No, I haven't met them. They aren't home. He keeps them at school, twenty-four-seven."

It was hard to keep resentment out of my voice. I couldn't shake the feeling that the Colonel viewed his children as nothing more than a status symbol, the way he viewed a wife.

"Single men are not allowed to raise their children at home," Lievoa threw casually over her shoulder.

"Are you saying he couldn't, even if he wanted to?" That was news to me.

"Nope. By law, all children have to remain in the institution selected for them with the help of genetic aptitude tests, until the age of nine. You didn't know that?"

"No. This wasn't in the information booklet provided."

"Weird." She shrugged. "What *was* in that booklet, then?"

"Well, the geographical maps of Neron and the country of Voran. The size of the population and forms of government. Your main industries. Natural resources..."

"All *useful* stuff, it seems," she scoffed, with sarcasm. "Doesn't Grevar have something better in his home entertainment library?"

Maybe he did, but we hadn't talked about it yet because we hadn't talked much, at all.

While on my own, I'd found a channel with daily news briefings in Omni's data system, a channel that streamed weather updates, and the one with various financial market information. Mostly, I'd just searched for pictures of Voranians going about their everyday life. I liked looking at them, it entertained and educated me, and also made me feel less alone.

Lievoa gave me a long look.

"Grevar really should update and expand his entertainment library. He may not have much leisure time to enjoy it, but it doesn't mean that you wouldn't. Watching shows is a great way to learn about our life here, in Voran, too."

She turned to keep going, taking me through the crowd across the room.

"You were talking about the twins..." I reminded, eager to hear more about them. "And the way the children are brought up in Voran."

"Well, with a rare exception, most Voranians grow up in a child-rearing facility," she continued, slowing down in her progress through the room a bit. "Fathers work to support their families. So, it was decided generations ago that for the benefit of our society, a universal system was needed to rear all children. After the age of nine, the children can transition to a day school and live at home. Few fathers can make it happen, though, since most work outside of the house. Personally, I lived in school until I was sixteen. All of my brothers stayed past the age of nine, too."

"There are no private daycares or babysitters, then?"

"No. The universal system is the only way the government can ensure a consistent quality of education and equal healthcare for all children. Maintaining the adequate re-population of our country is a matter of global importance, which makes every child extremely precious, you know."

"I see."

"Voran is a great place to be a woman, too. Lots of opportunities and a ton of admirers." She giggled, then grabbed my arm, shoving me forward. "And here we are."

I found myself in front of a colorful group of four women, who lingered next to a mobile buffet stand. Three of the four appeared to be at various stages of pregnancy.

All four turned to us, eyeing me with interest.

"The new Madam Colonel Kyradus, ladies," Lievoa introduced me in a sing-song voice.

"Just Daisy, please," I added with a smile, curious to meet some Voranian women at last.

Lievoa quickly said all their names and their husbands' titles to me, which I knew I might not remember from the first try. No one kissed me on the mouth, this time. That form of greeting must be reserved only for family members then, I realized with relief.

"And Madam Governor Drustan, herself." Lievoa gestured dramatically at the tall woman who seemed to be dominating the group.

Her green-and-purple dress streamed over her heavily pregnant belly, the fabric had an iridescent sheen to it, like peacock feathers. Clusters of colorful baubles dripped from her neck, ears, and horns, making me finally feel like I was not that overdressed with all the jewelry that the Colonel had decorated me with.

"Women can call me Shula," she said in a deep, velvety voice, dismissing Lievoa's formalities with a graceful gesture of a heavily bejeweled hand. Like her husband's, Shula's eyes were also yellow. Only unlike the Governor's lemon-light color, hers were dark gold.

"I trust your journey to Neron was good?" one of the women who flanked Shula asked. I believed Lievoa had introduced her as Iriha.

"Pretty uneventful." I shrugged, with a smile. "I spent most of it in cryo sleep."

"What was that like?" the other woman chimed in, her purple eyes open wide in wonder.

"I can't tell. I felt nothing at all. Waking up was a bit fuzzy at first, though."

"Do you like being married to the Colonel Kyradus?" Iriha asked. "He is a highly esteemed war hero, but I don't know much about him. He's rather unsociable."

"I find him a bit rough around the edges," the third woman added.

"You got that right," I muttered under my breath.

Shula winced, rubbing her belly.

"Kicking, again?" Iriha asked, sympathetically.

"A lot lately." Shula nodded.

"When is the baby due?" I asked cheerfully, joy for her shined in me. Waiting for a new baby's arrival must be even more exciting than waiting for Christmas morning.

"Any time next week." Shula leaned back a little then side to side, stretching her spine. "And it's three babies, not just one."

"Three?" I fisted my hands at my side, holding back from reaching out to pet her belly. I knew not all women liked that, no matter how much I wished to feel one of her babies kick. "You and the Governor must be so excited."

"These aren't his." She shook her head, making the strings of baubles on her ears and horns sway.

"No?"

"These are the triplets of the Senator Phirnic," she explained. "Three boys. Ours may be next, but we haven't decided yet."

Right, I should've known there would be a possibility of her carrying children of someone else. That was a part of the Voranian culture—married women helped single men start families through artificial insemination.

"How many children have you given birth to? If you don't mind my asking, of course," I added quickly.

"This is my third pregnancy," Shula replied with obvious pride.

"It's fascinating, and so kind of you to help the senator and the others with creating their families."

She slid me a measuring stare, her golden-yellow eyes assessing and calculating.

"Isn't that every woman's main duty and privilege? To bear children and populate their world?"

Well, personally I wouldn't say "every woman." On Earth, plenty of people of either gender found their life purpose beyond reproduction. The word "duty" sounded a bit off to me, too. However, I didn't come here to push my ways but to learn theirs. Besides, despite asking the questions, Shula's tone did not invite a debate.

So, I just muttered a non-definitive, "I suppose, so... In a way."

"Even with the Liaison Marriage Program being put in place," Shula continued, "the population growth in our country falls entirely on the Voranian women. Human females cannot be bred."

Being of different species, Voranians and humans couldn't reproduce. This had been proven in a lab already. I couldn't immediately tell whether she simply stated a fact or meant to offend me in some way.

"Well, there is more to a person than their ability to produce children, right?"

"Possibly." She shrugged.

"Oh, come on, Shula." Lievoa rolled her eyes. "All of us have plenty of interests other than pregnancies and labor. That's not what defines a person, and that's not why we're friends."

"I'm not talking about friends." Shula didn't spare Lievoa a glance, keeping her eyes on me. "This is about the value of a woman to her husband. What use is a wife who can never produce offspring?"

That was harsh. Her words and attitude no longer left any doubt—she meant to offend. She basically implied I would be useless to a Voranian husband, even if we managed to build a loving and carrying relationship. I forgot all about my diplomatic intentions. My blood heated with anger from the insult.

"You've got a celebrated war hero for a husband." She wouldn't quit. "He worked hard to get where he is, he literally risked his life for his status and position. What are *you* bringing to this marriage?"

I felt ill equipped to fight this battle—I had no loving relationship of my own to defend. Instead, I focused on an inter-species marriage in general.

"I could think of many benefits in having someone to share your life with," I said.

She pursed her lips. "Are you talking about sex?"

"Shula! That's mean." Lievoa grabbed my arm. "Let's go, Daisy."

Maybe I should've listened to her, but I couldn't leave it like that. Part of me couldn't accept someone being this condescending to me, someone I'd just met and hadn't given any reason to dislike me. At least I believed, I hadn't.

"I'm definitely not talking *just* about sex!" I felt my cheeks flame up with indignation, my face must be displaying all my feelings as usual.

"Then, you have completely lost me." Shula remained infuriatingly calm, her voice taunting.

Suddenly, she stepped closer to me. Wedging her shoulder between Lievoa and me, she leaned in to my ear.

"How can you truly share his life if you don't share his background or his culture?" She hissed low, just for me to hear. "You have to rely on a machine to even understand what he is saying. How can you possibly build the connection necessary for a successful life-long union? The only use for a wife like you could be sex, at most. Not unlike the pleasure machines in the mall."

That was an outright insult. My vision blurred from the offence. My breathing grew shallow and my hands trembled.

"Are you saying I could be nothing more but a sex toy to my husband?"

"Exactly." She kept her voice down. It occurred to me that she must know her behavior was unbecoming of her status, and therefore didn't want witnesses to our conversation. "Have no illusion, you're nothing but a glorified sex toy to him," she continued. "That is, if he finds you physically attractive. Though, *he* probably would fuck you either way. It wouldn't be like Grevar to play a gentleman when there is a willing woman in his bed. He is too wild to rein in his urges. Devastatingly handsome, rough, and so delightfully untamed..." Her voice turned into a dreamy murmur before trailing off as her gaze drifted aside somewhere.

Following her gaze, I saw it land on the Colonel across the room. He was still talking to the same group of men. They'd been joined by Governor Drustan, Shula's husband, but her attention was definitely on mine.

As if sensing Shula's stare, the Colonel turned over his shoulder. Meeting her eyes briefly, he gave her a deep, respectful nod.

"The one I've been with liked me just the way I am, 'rough and boorish.' Especially in the bedroom." The words he had tossed at me during our last argument sounded in my ears.

Could Shula be the one he'd been talking about? She sounded like she was very familiar with the Colonel's ways in the bedroom—more than I was, despite being his wife.

"What's that?" Shula tilted her head, obviously catching the shift in my expression. More than anything at that moment, I wished I'd mastered a poker face at some point in my life. "He hasn't fucked you, has he? After all this time having you in his house, he hasn't touched you." A crooked smile of satisfaction spread on her face. "He didn't find you to his taste, after all."

She'd guessed correctly. There hadn't been any true intimacy between the Colonel and I, and now there was never going to be since I was leaving him soon. This was a bitter reminder of what a sham my marriage had turned out to be.

Shula's obvious delight hurt, and it proved to be the last straw for me.

My anger boiled over.

"Oh, we've fucked," I said, loud and clear, for all the women around us to hear. "We've fucked so much and so hard, I had no energy left to even leave the house all this time—the glorified *sex doll* that I am as you said. He is a wild beast, indeed, definitely worth pining over for years. And trust me," I leaned forward as if about to reveal a secret. "As great as he might've been before, he's only gotten better—rough, wild, insatiable, and still very much untamed."

Shula narrowed her eyes at me, pressing her mouth together so tight, her lips all but disappeared. Then her gaze darted up over my shoulders, and her expression softened.

"Is everything okay, Daisy?" I felt the Colonel's hand on the small of my back.

"Hi." I glanced up at him. For once, his sudden appearance brought relief instead of tension. I was genuinely glad to see him, though he looked as grumpy as ever.

His brows knitted into a frown, he moved his stare from me to Shula, and I wondered if he'd heard any of my lies. Mortification spread hot through me at the thought.

"Grevar," Shula murmured breathlessly, betraying how much she still wanted him. "How so very nice to see you again. Madam Colonel was just telling us how deeply you've fallen in love in just a few days. I'm so happy for you."

His hand on my back jerked slightly, and I stiffened waiting for him to speak and expose me.

"Thank you." His arm slid around my waist as he drew me into his side. "Daisy proved irresistible, I stood no chance."

He leaned over, unexpectedly placing a kiss on my temple.

"Ladies." The Colonel tipped his head in a bow to the women. "Madam Governor." He turned to Shula who stood there, speechless. "I'm afraid I'll have to steal my wife from you. The Governor insists on seeing her again before we leave tonight."

A flock of warm tingles danced wildly inside me as he led me away.

Chapter 10

"GRAB A SHAWL!" THE Colonel shouted from the bottom of the stairs. "It's snowing outside."

"Colonel Kyradus would like you to wear a shawl," Omni forwarded to me in the bedroom.

"I heard him." I dashed to the closet and grabbed a white fuzzy wrap from one of the shelves. "The whole Voran must've heard him yelling, with that booming voice of his," I muttered, trotting down the stairs.

"Ready?" The Colonel took the shawl from my hands and wrapped it around my shoulders.

It'd been a week since my arrival in Voran. My first follow-up meeting with the Liaison Committee was scheduled for this morning.

The Colonel volunteered to come with me, possibly just to make sure I wasn't going to blabber something about our arrangement to anyone. Even so, I was glad to have him with me for support. Being questioned about my personal life wouldn't be fun, even if not much *personal* had happened to speak of.

"Let's go." His hand on the small of my back, he led me out to the landing platform.

"Oh, it's so beautiful!" I tilted my head back, watching the big, fluffy snowflakes flutter to the glass of the dome above us. Rushing around while getting ready upstairs earlier this morning, I had no chance to admire it.

"You've never seen snow before?" the Colonel asked, watching me while I was watching the leisurely snowfall.

"I have. But isn't it always so mesmerizing? Almost magical, like in a fairy tale?"

"Beautiful," he agreed, still gazing at *me*, not the snow.

The warm expression in his eyes wasn't entirely new. I'd caught him glancing at me with similar interest and awareness on one or two occasions lately. This time, however, it wasn't a mere glance. He stared at me openly, and I had no idea what to do about the warm, fuzzy feeling unfurling in my chest in response.

"Well, we'd better go," I mumbled, heading for the aircraft. "We don't want to keep Nancy and Alcus waiting."

It was weird and wonderful to watch the snowfall through the glass of the aircraft while I was dressed in a sleeveless summer dress under my shawl. Voranians, as I'd learned early on, loved green grass and flowers. They brought the summer indoors to enjoy it year around, ignoring the winter completely. All living and public spaces were enclosed under humongous glass domes. One didn't even have to own any winter clothes, as there was no need to go outside at all. Everywhere, the temperature was maintained at pretty much the same level.

I was wearing my booties, however, not wanting to shock Voranians with the sight of my feet.

"That's the Military Academy." The Colonel pointed at the rounded glass contraptions gracing the top of a sprawling building we were flying over. "The school where my boys are."

I remembered what Lievoa told me about the Voranian's laws in regards to children.

"You don't get to see them often."

"At least one weekend a month. Sometimes more often, depending on their educational plan and my work obligations."

"It must be hard."

A family I used to babysit for had moved to another town shortly before I had to leave for Neron. I missed the children I'd worked with, and those weren't even *my* children.

The Colonel didn't speak about his sons often, though. This was the first time he'd mentioned them since that unfortunate dinner.

"Do you...miss them?"

He rolled his wide shoulders back then turned away from me, as if to watch the snow outside the glass of the aircraft.

"I do." His throat bobbed with a swallow. His voice sounded rougher than usual. "I fly over their school to and from work, even though it's not on the way. It takes me an extra hour each day, but I often catch a glimpse of them doing their exercise in the morning or playing in the evening."

"When is your next visit with them?"

"This weekend." He cleared his throat, his tone lifting. "Five days from now."

I thought back to when he'd told me their full names.

"Olvar Shula Kyradus and Zun Shula Kyradus."

Both had *Shula* in them.

"Is it customary to have the mother's name as a child's middle name in Voran?" I asked.

"Yes," he replied.

"Is Shula, the Governor's wife, the mother of your children, then?"

There could very well be more than one Shula in the City of Voran, but somehow, I already knew that it was her.

"Yes."

On the way back from the Governor's Palace, the Colonel had asked me what Shula and I had been talking about at the ball, and I'd given him a very general reply.

I believed he'd heard me lying about our non-existent sex life to her, and I was afraid he'd bring it up if I told him about Shula's comments. Frankly, I also felt embarrassed for her, and had no desire to repeat her words to him or anyone else.

Now, everything had come together.

"Let me guess." I drew in a long breath. "Your sons were *not* conceived by artificial insemination?"

"No. Shula and I used to be lovers."

My heart squeezed with a sudden ache. Why would the Colonel's history with another woman bother me? None of it was my business. It did not concern me at all.

"Was she the Governor's wife already?" I couldn't stop myself, needing to know more. All of it. "When you..."

"Of course not," he glared at me, indignantly. "Drustan has been my friend since the academy. I would've never had sex with Shula had she been his wife already. In fact, I met her first."

"You did?"

His chest rose as he inhaled deeply. "I was the one who introduced her to him."

"So, the Governor ended up stealing your woman?" I blurted out.

Having met Shula, I wondered if the Colonel actually got lucky by dodging *that* bullet. But if he was still hurting over her... Compassion for him stirred inside me.

"There was no *stealing*." The Colonel shook his head. "Drustan went about it in a fair, honest way—that's why we're still friends. He proposed to Shula the same year I did. She chose him."

"Why?"

I found Governor Drustan pleasant enough, but I remembered how Shula had gazed at the Colonel at the ball, with longing and maybe even some regret.

"It was nearly six years ago, Daisy. I was an Army Captain, about to be shipped off to a war I might not return from. Drustan was a rising-star politician, with brilliant career prospects ahead of him. Shula made her choice."

"I bet she's regretting it, now that you're still very much alive and the Colonel of the Army to boot," I said, not without a hint of schadenfreude.

"Shula is happy with Drustan," he replied firmly. "As his wife, she is the highest-placed woman in Voran. He has given her everything she's ever wanted and more."

"If you say so."

Why would she eye someone else's husband with so much longing, then? If she got everything she'd ever wanted from her own?

I didn't tell that to him, of course. Instead, I searched for something else to say to him, something that would preferably make him forget all about that woman. Only, there was no forgetting her. She was the mother of his children, who had refused to be his wife.

"I'm sorry, Colonel."

"Don't be. It's absolutely normal in Voran," he said calmly. "Shula got eleven marriage proposals that year, including Drustan's and mine. No matter whom she chose, ten men had to be rejected. An average Voranian man proposes many times during his lifetime and is still likely to remain single at the end."

"How many times have you proposed?"

He glanced out the window again.

"Once was enough for me."

Not sure what else to say to cheer him up at this point, I silently reached over and took his hand in mine. His holding my hand earlier had been nice and comforting. I hoped he'd feel my support for him now, too.

THE COMMITTEE MEETING turned out to be more boring and less stressful than I'd anticipated.

The Colonel held my hand as a doting husband would. I batted my eyelashes at him, convincing both humans and Voranians that we had been getting along splendidly.

I tried not to overdo it, though, since merely three weeks from now, the Colonel and I would be coming to the very same building to petition the same group of people to dissolve our marriage and take me back to Earth. With the Colonel's support, however, I believed it would be possible to make it happen.

The rest of the week went fairly smoothly. The Colonel and I had fallen into a routine that seemed to work for both of us. He left for work while I was still in bed. I spent the day exploring Omni's entertainment library—updated and much expanded through the efforts of Lievoa, who'd send me copious amounts of interesting pictures, fun shows, and useful documentaries on Voranian life. I also learned from Omni the Aldraian technique of taking care of plants. The dwellers of the nearby planet, Aldrai, were considered the top experts in horticulture in this part of the Galaxy. I'd learned that Aldraians literally lived in their gardens—they built no houses.

Whenever I could, I also continued experimenting with baking in the kitchen. The Colonel was still refusing to let me leave the house on my own, which irked me immensely. I couldn't order all the ingredients through Omni. It was impossible to determine what I needed without me being able to touch, taste, and smell things to figure out what I could substitute with them in my recipes.

He stubbornly refused to understand that, which resulted in a few more blow-outs between us. This man could get my blood boiling by hardly saying anything at all.

Thankfully, he had been making visible efforts to control his temper, which I appreciated, and I tried to watch my own moods in return. That had made our arguments shorter, less explosive, and less upsetting for both of us.

The upcoming weekend, the Colonel was going to be off work, so he arranged to spend one entire day at the Military Academy with the twins.

The day before that, the two of us had dinner in his gorgeous dining room.

"What is this?" I stared at the deep bowl Omni had placed in front of me as soon as I'd taken my seat.

About a dozen gray leech-like worms swarmed in the black water inside the bowl, making my stomach roil.

"They are called *recols*, Madam Kyradus."

"I felt like celebrating tonight," the Colonel smiled brightly across the table, an identical bowl stood in front of him.

"Celebrating? With these?" I tried hard not to look at the slimy things stretching and coiling in my bowl. "How? What do you do with them?"

Flush them down the toilet, what I would do.

"You eat them." The Colonel's smile grew wider.

"*Recols* are a rare delicacy from the underwater caves of Aldrai," Omni declared. I could have sworn I heard a note of delight in his mechanical voice, too. "Extremely difficult to catch and astronomically expensive."

"The expense is worth it." The Colonel appeared to be in an exceptionally good mood tonight, and I believed it had everything to do with him looking forward to seeing his kids tomorrow.

I understood his desire to celebrate that. But worms?

Why worms?

"Enjoy." He fished one out of the bowl with his fingers. The thing stretched and curled its soft body around one of the Colonel's claws as he lifted it to his mouth.

"Oh God..." I stared at him in shock. "You're not going to..."

My stomach lurched as he put the pale leech-thing into his mouth. Shoving the chair away from the table, I dashed for the closest washroom.

"Daisy?" The Colonel's hooves thundered against the tiled floor as he rushed after me.

I managed to shut the bathroom door in his face, dropping to my knees in front of the toilet before my stomach emptied itself into it.

"God, this was nasty," I groaned, trying to get the image of the worm wiggling in the Colonel's fingers out of my head.

"Daisy!" He slammed something heavy against the bathroom door—his fist or possibly his hoof, maybe both.

"Just...give me a minute." I rinsed my mouth then washed my face.

"Are you okay?" he called from behind the door. "Tell me or I'm breaking in!"

"Fine. I'm fine." I drank some water from the tap then opened the door, finally feeling ready to face him again.

"Daisy." He grabbed me by my upper arms, staring at my face intently. "What happened? Are you ill?" He slid his hands up, cupping my face. "You look more colorless than usual."

"Thanks." I smiled at the way he put it.

The fur on the back of his hands softly tickled the base of my neck as he inspected my face. The concern in his eyes was genuine, and I liked that way too much—he truly cared. "I'm good, now, I promise."

My smile eased the worry on his face.

"Was something wrong with the *recols*?" he asked.

Was anything right about those things? Even their name reminded me of the word "recoil." How fitting.

"Sorry, I didn't mean to spoil your celebration, but I don't think I can ever eat those... I would prefer not to watch you eat them, either." A shudder ran through my entire body. "Please?"

He dropped his hands from my face to my shoulders but didn't remove them from me, and I liked that more than I should have. I loved the feel of his warm, large hands on me.

"Earthlings don't have foods like that?" he asked.

"Oh God, no!" I shook my head quickly, then thought about it more carefully. "Well, there are fried crickets, but they would be already dead when you eat them. Lobsters are boiled alive, which is kind of icky when you think about it. Oh, and raw oysters. Some find those really gross... They're alive when you eat them, but they don't wiggle."

"So, the *recols'* moving was what upset you?"

I touched his hand on my shoulder, stroking his short fur on it the way I used to pet my cat. It felt similarly comforting.

"I think it's the whole package, to be honest—their shape, their color, and yes, their wiggling too."

"I didn't order the *recols* to upset you," he explained, and I believed him. "I didn't expect you to react this way."

"I understand. Promise not to hold it against you." I smiled again.

I wasn't upset with him, not at all, but I wouldn't go anywhere near those things again.

He stared at me for a brief moment, his intense gaze lingering on my smiling lips.

"Come, we'll eat something else." Finally taking his hands off me, he stepped back, and I leaned after him involuntarily, as if drawn by some gravitational field toward him. "I want us to have dinner together."

"Sure. As long as it's something less wiggly, please." I followed him back to the dining room.

The bowls with the slimy creatures had been thankfully removed from the table. The usual checkered trays stood in their place.

"I'm sorry. You said those things were expensive," I said. "I hope they don't go to waste."

He huffed a laugh. "Don't worry. I'll have a most decadent lunch at work, next week. The entire office will be drooling."

"Are they really such a delicacy?"

He lifted an eyebrow, giving me a lop-sided grin. "Insanely self-indulgent."

"I'm sorry I couldn't appreciate that."

"Stop apologizing." He shrugged, tossing a piece of meat into his mouth. "I'm sure there would be more than one thing I'd find repulsive about Earth, too."

"Well, all those human toes, for one!" I laughed and he joined me.

"Toes aren't that bad." He shook his head. "I could absolutely get used to seeing them."

I crossed my feet in pale-pink ballet flats under the table.

"Does it mean I can start running barefoot around here?" I teased.

"Um." His beard hid his smile, but I noticed the merry glimmer in his eyes. "Let's just start with sandals first."

"I have some peep-toe pumps in the closet." I giggled. "I can start by displaying one toe at a time."

Despite its rough beginning, this dinner turned out to be the best I'd had in the Colonel's house so far. It was most likely because of his better mood due to the upcoming visit with his children.

"Colonel, would it be okay if I came to see the boys with you, tomorrow?" I asked before giving myself any time to think it through.

The path of my words from first occurring in my brain to leaving my mouth had always been exceptionally short, which had cost me some rather embarrassing moments in the past. I had no right to demand to meet his family—I was leaving him in a couple of weeks. But he seemed relaxed tonight and more approachable than ever before, and I couldn't help it.

"You want to meet my sons?" he asked, his expression turning serious.

"Yes," I replied earnestly. "I'd love to. If you don't mind."

The twins were a big part of my reasons for coming to Neron. It would be incredibly sad to leave here without meeting them at all.

He seemed to consider it for a moment.

"We'll have them for about seven hours," he said, "from after breakfast until before dinner."

"So, I can come?" I perked up, my chest quickly filling with excitement ready to burst out.

"If it'll make you happy—"

"Oh, it will!" I jumped out of my chair and rushed to his side of the table. "Thank you!" I threw my arms around his neck impulsively.

With the Colonel sitting down, his head ended up pressed to my chest when I hugged him—his horns rising right in front of my face, his cheek squished into my breasts.

The strained sound of him clearing his throat brought me back to my senses, and I quickly released him from my hug.

"Um…" I scratched my ear, awkwardly retreating to my seat.

The lingering sensation of his beard stuffed into my cleavage rippled with awareness along my skin. I rubbed my chest, and he followed my gesture with his vivid red eyes.

What was it that we had been talking about? I had a hard time collecting my thoughts.

Of course, his children, for goodness sake!

"So, um… Will we be allowed to take the boys off the school property?"

He blinked, raising a hand to his cheek, the one that had just been shoved between my breasts. He then jerked his hand back quickly. "Yes. Where would you like to go?"

I thought back to my babysitting days. This time of the year, kids loved to play in the snow, and we had plenty of it in Voran after the recent snowfall. I wondered if Voranians built snowmen, or knew how to make snow angels.

"Do the boys have warm clothes, to go outside?" I asked.

"Why?"

"I thought we could take them to an outdoor park somewhere. Do you have outdoor places, where children can run and play freely? We all could play in the snow for a little bit. Or do Voranians never go outside of their glass domes?"

"We do. We go outside in the summer, all the time," the Colonel assured me.

"How about in the winter?"

"Only if we have to. The Military Academy has outdoor training on the curriculum. I've gone through many outdoor survival courses, in all conditions—"

"Oh, but the outdoors can be *enjoyed*, not just survived." I clutched my hands at my chest. "Even if you don't do any winter sports, snow can be so much fun."

He stared at me for a moment, with a hint of a smile hiding in the depths of his beard.

"Fine," he repeated my favorite word. "Let's go outside."

Chapter 11

I BOUNCED ON THE HEELS of my fur-trimmed boots, standing on the grass-covered roof of the main building of The Military Academy. It was warm here, under the giant dome, but a fluffy winter coat was waiting for me in the Colonel's aircraft, along with a scruffy fur coat for him and the kids' winter clothes.

"Where are they?" I muttered impatiently. "How much longer?"

As a part of the large group of parents—mostly dads—the Colonel and I lined up along the entire circumference of the roof area, waiting for the children to be released to us.

"What's taking them so long?" I asked impatiently, doing my best to ignore the stares of the fathers and the staff alike.

As one of a handful of women under the dome and the only human, I attracted a lot of attention. The ogling would make me uncomfortable had it not been for the anticipation of meeting the two little guys soon. It kept my focus off the crowd and their scrutiny.

"Soon." The Colonel patted my arm in a calming gesture. "They have a number of protocols to follow before the children can be released." He shifted his weight to his other hoof. "May I request something from you?"

"Sure. What is it?" I glanced at him.

His expression, even more serious than usual, made me pause.

"I prefer not to introduce you to my children as my wife," he said. "I don't want them to know that we're married."

I had no plans to tell them that anyway, of course, but something inside me deflated at his request. As if a piece of my excitement had chipped away with this reminder of how things really were between us.

"But wouldn't the children know that already?" The entire country knew.

"According to the rules of The Ministry of Children's Education and Wellbeing, all family news is to be delivered to students by close family members, unless instructed otherwise."

"And you have never told them?" It'd been months since he'd learned about me.

"No. I wanted to meet you in person first."

I didn't blame him for wanting to protect his children.

"Do they know that I'm here, at all?"

"No. I was going to tell them later, after—" He stopped himself. "Well, after you would've settled."

But I hadn't. I hadn't settled into my role of his wife and his children's stepmom as the whole world had expected me to do. At this point, I wasn't even their nanny. As far as the children would ever know, I was a nobody—a random visitor from another planet, who would be gone from their lives by the time of their dad's next visit here.

All of it felt so excruciatingly sad.

Yes, my husband was…difficult at times. Not counting that initial burst of lust, the only feelings he'd expressed toward me had been those of duty and obligation. This marriage was nothing more than a status symbol to him and empty misguided hopes for me. But I wondered what would've happened had we tried hard enough to make it work.

Right now, it felt like we hadn't tried at all.

"It's fine," I said to him. "I understand. You have nothing to worry about. I'm just visiting here."

He watched me carefully for another moment, then opened his mouth as if about to say something.

The wide sliding doors on the opposite end of the dome finally opened, and several columns of little Voranians marched out. Arranged by height, from the shortest to the tallest, a few hundred children filled the grassy space under the dome.

Walking in sync, they maintained perfect order, like a true military parade. Until about halfway through. Once the kids started spotting their dads in the crowd of parents, the rows and columns wavered then broke apart.

"Dad! Daddy!" seemed to come from everywhere at once, as children ran to their parents.

"There they are!" The Colonel grinned, stepping forward then taking off in a jog toward the approaching children.

Two little fur balls in gray uniforms separated from the crowd, dashing his way.

"Daddy!"

He caught them, each in one arm, then took them for a spin a few times. Their little arms wrapped around his thick neck, they giggled and covered his face with kisses.

My heart melted and ached at seeing them together like that, and I pressed my hands to my chest, struggling to hold it together.

"I've brought someone who wants to meet you." He set the boys down on the ground, tilting his horns my way.

The kids let go of him, staring at me with two pairs of wide-open eyes.

"What's this?" one asked, taking a tentative step my way.

"Not *what*! Olvar, where are your manners?" The Colonel looked mortified, and I laughed.

"My name is Daisy." I crouched down to bring myself to their eye level.

"Are you a girl?" The other one shifted hoof to hoof next to his brother. Their little uniforms were almost identical to that of their father, gray with gold-and-red trim. Instead of his impressive epaulettes, however, they had narrow stripes of gold on their shoulders.

"A woman," the Colonel corrected. "And I demand you two treat Daisy with respect."

"Yes, father," they said in unison.

Being an identical copy of each other, they would be impossible to tell apart. However, I noticed that their eye color was different. Olvar's eyes were bright red, just like their dad's. Zun's were vivid orange, which was the mix of the Colonel's red with the golden-yellow of their mother's.

"I'm so happy your dad brought me along today." I smiled, offering my hand to Olvar, who happened to be a little closer to me. He appeared to be a bit more daring than his brother. "It's very nice to meet you."

With a serious expression on his face, the boy took my hand in both of his, lowering his head in a perfectly executed formal bow.

"It's nice to meet you too, Madam..." He gave his father a questioning look, as if enquiring about the proper form of addressing me.

"Daisy," I rushed out. "Just call me Daisy, please."

"What's a *daisy*?"

"It's the name of a flower from Earth, the planet I come from. But it's also my first name."

"Are you a grownup? Because it's not proper to address a grownup by their first name, unless they're a family. Are you a family?"

The Colonel's brief cough sounded from the side.

"I'm a friend," I said to Olvar quickly. "Friends call each other by their first names, don't they? You'll call me Daisy, and I'll call you Olvar. Deal?"

He blinked, glancing at his father then back at me again.

"Deal." He nodded somberly, shaking my hand between his two.

"And you must be Zun?" I offered my hand to the second boy, who lingered behind his brother.

"Yeah..." He scratched his shoulder.

"Zun." Olvar shoved an elbow into his brother's side.

"Oh, um." Zun came closer to me, grabbing my hand with both of his in the Voranian greeting. "I am very pleased to meet you...Daisy."

"Great." I fluffed the fur on the back of his hand with my other hand. Zun's fur was much finer than his father's. It stood up on top of his head and curled above his ears in the same fashion as his brother's. "Guess what we're going to do, now?"

"What?" Zun tilted his head to the side, pulling at his ear. Curiosity shone in his bright orange eyes.

"We're going outside." I smiled.

"Where outside?" Olvar hopped closer. So close, I had to shuffle backwards in my crouch, lest he stab me with his little horns in excitement.

"You'll see." Compared to the Colonel's, their horns were tiny, barely three inches long, if that. I noticed a ring of characters carved on Olvar's right horn. His brother had a similar design, too. "What does the writing on your horn mean?"

"*Olvar Shula Kyradus. Cadet #397576-H of the Voran Military Academy*," he recited proudly, without tripping over the long number.

"Dad has more," Zun pointed out.

With a kind expression in his eyes, the Colonel ruffled the fuzzy fur on his son's head.

"Those chosen for a military career get their first carving shortly after birth." He took Zun's hand in his right hand, catching Olvar's with his left, then led all of us toward the parking hangar. "As the career and rank advance, the record expands."

Walking next to him, I studied the long spiral of carvings on his right horn. It started from about three inches from the top, swirling down to the base, with barely a sliver of clean space visible above the fur on his head.

"What happens if you run out of space?"

"The horns grow. Much slower with age, though. The trick is to rise through the ranks at the same rate as the horns grow, I guess." He laughed. The deep sound pleasantly resonated through my chest.

"Could there be some electronic records, instead?" I asked.

"There are. This is just an old tradition to publicly display one's accomplishments," he said, then added casually, "And a good way to identify a dead body of a soldier fallen on a battlefield. Especially if the rest of him has been destroyed beyond recognition."

"Dead?" I gaped at him then glanced at the children.

He intercepted my gaze.

"My sons are future soldiers, Daisy. They're aware of the risks that come with their occupation."

"Are you okay with that?"

"If there is an untimely death in their future, I can only hope it'll come with honor and dignity. We all die, sooner or later. An honorable death on a battlefield is better than many others."

"OH NO!" I DUCKED, AVOIDING a snow ball thrown my way. "I need a break."

Panting hard from running through snowdrifts in the deserted outdoor park, I plopped on my butt into the nearest snowbank. I'd laughed so much this morning, my facial muscles started cramping.

"Daisy!" The boys crushed into me at full speed, knocking me backwards. "We're not done yet."

"Ten minutes, guys, please," I begged. "I'll come finish your fort with you right after I catch my breath. Promise."

"Come, gentlemen." The Colonel ripped them both off me. "We'll start another wall for the fort while the lady regains her strength."

As soon as their father set them down, Olvar kicked his hoof up, spraying his brother with snow.

"Hey!" Zun leaped aside, adjusting his hat that kept sliding over his eyes, even though it was held by his horns sticking through the holes in the top. Zun stuck his tongue out at his brother. "Maaah."

My jaw dropped. "Wow!"

Dark-red and tapered at the end, his tongue must've been at least twice as long as mine.

"That is quite a tongue you have there, mister—" I stopped myself quickly, realizing that wasn't what I should be focusing on. "That's not the way to treat your brother, by the way."

"I have a tongue like that, too!" Olvar jumped in, opening his mouth and rolling his tongue out. I never knew that Voranians typically had those organs that long.

"Show us yours!" The boys hopped around me. "Show us!"

"Well, it's not really polite to stick your tongue out at people."

"Please! Please!"

"Okay, just this once." I swallowed, then opened my mouth to display my inadequate organ to them. I stretched it down as far as I could, wiggling the end.

"It's pink!" Olvar gasped.

"And so short." Zun gazed at it then at me, compassion spreading on his cute little face. "Did somebody cut it for you?"

"No!" I laughed. "I was born like this. All people on Earth have shorter tongues than Voranians, it seems."

"Daddy's tongue is the longest," Olvar proudly informed me. "Show her, Dad."

Obviously discomfited by the request, the Colonel cleared his throat.

"Oh, it's fine..." I started to protest.

But he'd already opened his mouth, rolling out the tongue that actually reached his chest.

"See? See?" The boys elbowed me. "Isn't Dad's the longest tongue ever?"

"Well, yes, that's..." The smile slipped off my face as the thought of what it would feel like to kiss him unexpectedly entered my mind.

It went downhill from there. Way, way *down*. I shifted in the snow, forcing myself not to think about all the wonderful things he could probably do with that tongue of his.

"All right, boys." The Colonel shoo-ed them toward the snow-covered area that we had barely touched yet. A good part of the park had already been covered with snow angels and snowmen.

"I'll hold them off for ten minutes. Be ready, they'll come for you, then," he told me before leaving to follow his sons.

I watched the three of them stomp out the snow along the perimeter of the new section of the fort we'd started building together. They then began erecting the walls from snow balls that they rolled around to make bigger. The Colonel propped two huge ones on each end of the wall. He then started carefully arranging the much smaller ones that his children made for him.

He had infinite patience when dealing with his sons, explaining and showing them how to do things as many times as was needed until they got it right.

Knowing his explosive temper, I was shocked he hadn't once raised his voice at the boys. Not that he needed to. His kids seemed to read him well. They would stop their horsing around the moment he'd give them a stern look.

"Ten minutes are up!" Olvar ran back, collapsing into the snow in front of me. His brother tumbled right over him.

"Shall we go, then?" I clapped my hands, shaking off the snow from my mittens. "Get that fort done?"

"No, I'm tired of fort building." Zun rolled to his back, spreading his arms wide to make another snow angel.

"Come on." Olvar nudged his brother with his horns. "I'll roll *you* into a ball!" He grabbed Zun and rolled him in the snow. "I'll make you into a tower for our fort."

"Um..." I moved to intervene.

"He'll be fine." The Colonel stopped me with his hand on my shoulder.

"Are you sure?" I watched the two of them tumble down a small hill, giggling and kicking their hooves.

"Absolutely." He sat in the snow next to me. "What's the worst that can happen?"

"Well—"

"That was a rhetorical question," he stopped me from replying. "As a parent, I have a list as long as my tail of all the horrible things that could possibly happen to my children at any given minute. I just try not to fret over that or project my fears onto them. Let them be kids."

I settled back into the snow, folding my hands in my lap.

"What is the mother's role in the upbringing of her children in Voran?" I asked.

"A minimal one. Unless they're the children of her husband." He placed his forearms on his bent knees. "All parental rights go to the father if he is not married to the mother. It enables a woman to have more children if fewer responsibilities are attached with each of them."

"I see."

I brushed some snow off my white coat over my knee.

"Colonel..." I started, feeling a need to apologize. "I'm sorry I've accused you of being a bad parent."

He huffed a laugh.

"That hasn't been the only thing you've accused me of."

I cast a furtive glance his way, relieved to see he didn't seem offended. His expression remained relaxed, happy even.

"Well, some of that has been true. Don't you agree?" I lifted an eyebrow. "Admit it, Omni had to clean an insane amount of broken glass in the first couple of days."

"True." He had the decency to look ashamed. "I'm sorry, too."

"I love hearing this word from you." I turned my face to him with a smile. "It's music to my ears."

Tipping his head back, he laughed out loud. A deep and hearty sound. It proved highly contagious as I couldn't hold back a laugh, too.

After sitting in the snow for a while, I felt the cold sneaking under my warm clothes. I took my mitts off, rubbing my hands to warm them up.

"Cold?" he asked, taking his gloves off, too.

"A little."

"Come here." He shifted closer, taking my chilled hands in his big and still surprisingly warm ones.

"Thank you. I wish I had some fur on the back of my hands, too. It must keep your hands warm, in addition to the gloves?"

He appeared distracted, not replying right away.

"Daisy," he said, rubbing my hands between his. "Would you reconsider leaving when the month is up? You said earlier that you might."

"Well, I..." His request caught me off guard.

A lot had changed since I'd first negotiated with him the conditions of my leaving Voran. Living under the same roof with the Colonel had certainly become less stressful. Could I stay longer than a month? A year, like I had planned?

Who could say what the upcoming year would bring, though?

I retrieved my hands from him and slid the mitts back on.

"My work doesn't allow me to have the boys home every weekend," the Colonel continued before I could come up with an answer.

"You told me it was also because of their educational plan."

"That, too." He nodded. "However, some families obtain permission to take their children home every weekend."

"How?"

"Parents can take a course on the nutritional and educational requirements for their children. As long as they pass the exam and take the regular refresher courses to ensure they maintain the school's standards at home, they're allowed to take their children every weekend."

"Why didn't you take the course, then?"

"I did. But it's much harder for me to obtain permission. In my position, I can be called to work or even picked up from home, in case of an emergency, any minute of the day. The law doesn't allow leaving small children unattended, not that I would do that anyway."

"I understand." It was illegal in many countries on Earth, too.

It sounded like the Colonel could really benefit from having a live-in nanny. Except that the Voranian law didn't permit that.

He turned to me, searching my eyes.

"Daisy, would you agree to take the course and stay for the entire year?" he said in one breath.

With the children now being in the picture, my staying here made more sense.

The Colonel no longer scared me. However, a certain type of tension remained between us.

I no longer felt frightened or uncomfortable in his presence, but I couldn't fully relax either. Whenever he entered a room, my awareness would shift to him, attuning to his every word or movement.

Having him as my employer should clear things up, though, as we both would finally have clear roles to define our relationship. From now on, I'd be his nanny, and he'd be my boss.

I watched the boys chase each other through the snow, their short little tails whipping behind them, their laughter ringing through the chilly air.

"I most definitely could take the course." I nodded, staring at the kids playing in the snow, two pairs of horns glistening in the midday sun. "I'd love to help you look after these two."

The Colonel released a long breath.

"I can't believe my children have just succeeded where I have failed," he said with a smile in his deep voice.

I slid a suspicious glance at him. "Did you just use your kids to make me stay?"

"And it was worth it!" He grinned at me without a hint of remorse. "Hey boys! Olvar, Zun, guess what?"

"What?" They bounced our way.

"Daisy is staying for an entire year with us," he announced brightly, giving me a wink.

"A year!" They turned to me.

"Minus the two weeks that have passed," I added quickly.

The Colonel ignored my statement. "We'll be bringing you home every weekend."

The kids' jewel-colored eyes shone with delight that warmed my heart.

"Can we build snowmen every week?" Olvar asked.

"Well, as long as there is snow, I guess." I spread my hands aside.

"Yes!" They both leaped at me at once, pushing me back into the snow.

They giggled, making me laugh as I rolled in the snow with them.

The Colonel was right. It was definitely worth it.

Chapter 12

"WHERE IS THAT FUCKING thing!" the Colonel's deep voice boomed from downstairs. The sound of his stomping hooves echoed through the entire cluster of domes of his place.

With a last glance at my reflection in the mirror, I smoothed the flared skirt of my powder-blue dress, shoved my feet into a pair of cream-colored pumps and ran out of the bedroom.

It'd been over a week since our play day in the snow. My parenting course at The Ministry of Children's Education and Wellbeing had started yesterday. The Colonel was about to drop me off for my second class on his way to work.

"What are you looking for?" I asked, running down the stairs into the main room.

"My fucking personal tablet," he growled, shoving aside the flower garlands to search behind the pots by the wall. "I always put it right here!" He slammed his fist into one of the planters. "Every fucking morning. And now I'm going to be late for work!"

"Oh, you won't." I waved him off. "You're always a year early everywhere, anyway. Omni," I asked, turning to the frame on the stick quietly humming nearby. "Do you know where the Colonel's tablet went?"

"Unfortunately, that unit is not connected to my system. I am unable to locate it," the AI sounded crestfallen.

I knew the robot had no emotions, he simply mirrored the intonations of people, but I still felt sorry for him.

"Colonel Kyradus did not notify me of the tablet's location when he misplaced it," Omni added, apologetically.

"If I *knew* of its location to notify you then it wouldn't be misplaced in the first place," the Colonel raged. "Would it?"

"Didn't you go to the bathroom, after breakfast?" I dashed to the main floor bathroom.

Sure enough, the tablet was lying right there, behind the oblong flower pot next to the hand dryer by the sink.

Back in the main room, I shoved it into the Colonel's hands.

"Here. Stop stomping around and yelling at the poor robot. And don't forget to charge it in the aircraft on your way to work."

He grunted, staring at the tablet in his hands then moved his eyes to me.

"Why do I let you get away with chastising me as if I were a child, in front of my household AI nevertheless?"

I propped my hands on my hips.

"Because I'm pretty much the only person on this planet who is not afraid to tell you things the way they are."

There was no need for me to be afraid of him, I trusted the Colonel would never hurt me. I also sensed he appreciated hearing the truth from me.

I grabbed the bag with my own tablet and some writing materials off the hook by the door.

"Oh, and because you *like* me, of course," I teased, wishing to disperse the tension that was still hanging over him like a storm cloud.

His stare lingered on me, growing more intense. The tension in the air didn't dissipate but its nature seemed to shift somehow, chasing my smile away.

"Um, we should go," I said quietly, twisting the handle of my bag in my hands. "Now, you're actually risking being late."

He didn't move from his spot, however, continuing to stare at me.

"How are you feeling about the class today, Daisy?" he asked.

Yesterday, before it started, I'd felt sick with nerves.

I'd learned that at least half of the students in my class would be women. My encounter with Voranian women at the Governor's Ball hadn't gone that well, because of Shula, of course. She had given me a glimpse into how Earth females might be perceived in Voran, and I had *not* been looking forward to hearing more insults from anyone.

Thankfully, my worst fears hadn't been realized. Yesterday had gone pretty well. Sure, there had been stares and even a few whispers behind my back, but no one had dared insult me to my face. Most had actually made a visible effort to be nice to me.

"Are you sure you don't want me to have a talk with the instructor?" The Colonel glared from under his bushy eyebrows. "I can find some time to visit the classroom this morning. No one would dare to even think about treating you badly after I'm done with them."

"Oh, I know they wouldn't." I snorted a laugh when I imagined showing up to class on the arm of the big, mean Colonel. "Most would probably pee their pants at the sight of you." I wasn't even kidding about that one. The Colonel in a fit of rage was terrifying. I knew that for a fact.

"Everyone who disrespects you is disrespecting me," he snarled.

"Calm down." I patted his hand that was still holding the freaking tablet. "No one is disrespecting me. Everybody was courteous and polite. Oh, and one woman, her name is Diecrie, but the instructor was calling her Madam Judge Cistridus, she even told me how glad she was that the Voranian government moved ahead with the Liaison Program. Her father recently passed away. He was alone and lonely. She is hoping her three brothers will eventually earn the honor of having human wives to love and grow old with."

The Colonel took a step closer to me.

"You see, this here," he waved his hand between us, "it's bigger than you and me. It's a hope for many men in my country." He placed his hand on my shoulder then slid it down to circle my bare upper arm.

The warmth in his eyes heated slowly as he drew little circles on my skin with his thumb.

My arm tingled where his hand touched it, the sensation rippling downwards. The tension in the air now crackled with heat I had no idea what to do with. I felt like either running away from him or throwing myself at him and kissing the living hell out of him.

Neither scenario would be appropriate for what we now were—a boss and an employee. I had hoped that having clear roles would simplify our relationship. On the contrary, it'd only gotten more complicated.

An employer shouldn't be caressing his nanny's arms, and she shouldn't be enjoying every little physical contact with him as much as I was.

So, I dealt with the situation the only way I knew how, by making a stupid joke.

"Well, if Voranian men hope to get human wives, they'd better start getting used to the sight of human feet. The sooner they accept the fact that our women have toes, the less chance of them freaking out the way you did."

"Hey," his expression eased into a smile as he chuckled. "I don't mind your toes. You know I wouldn't say a word if you were to run around completely barefoot."

"You wouldn't? But that would deprive me of the chance to tease you. Besides, all the shoes you got for me are too cute to walk barefoot. Ooops..." I glanced at Omni's screen nearby, "now, we really need to hurry." I grabbed him under his arm, tugging him toward the parking platform. "Or we both will be late."

Once inside the aircraft, I decided he was in a decent enough mood this morning to bring up another subject. Again.

"Colonel, you must have noticed, I've been trying to make something in the kitchen," I started, carefully.

"Yes. What are you trying to do?" He connected his tablet to the control panel for re-charging.

"Baking. I want to figure out how to bake my recipes from home, using Voranians ingredients."

"Why? You don't like our desserts?"

That wasn't the point, but he had been so stubborn about this entire thing from the beginning.

"No, everything I've eaten in Voran so far has been tasty. Except for the *recols*, of course. Since my class ends at noon, I have an entire afternoon with nothing to do."

"You like to bake that much?" He glanced at me with curiosity.

No temper flare-ups, I noted, so far so good.

"It relaxes me," I explained. "Baking is something I've done since I was a little girl. My grandmother taught me how to bake, and it makes me happy. I love the creativity that goes into the decorating, too. I worked in a bakery for years before it closed for good. I've even dreamed of opening my own bakery one day, except that my salary never allowed for saving much to start my own business. Anyway, it was fun."

"Well, you know you have my permission to use anything in the house. Bake whatever you like. Tell Omni to get what you need."

And there it was again. I was allowed to do whatever I wanted, as long as I remained under the dome of his home, like a fly trapped under a glass.

"See, that's where the problem lies. I can't order what I don't know. I need to speak with someone who bakes in Voran, who sells the ingredients so they would point me in the right direction."

"You want to go to the spice market, then?"

That sounded promising.

"Is there such a thing?"

"Yes, in the mall. But I can't take you there, possibly until the end of the next week."

"Can't I go on my own?" I smiled as sweetly as I could, batting my lashes at him innocently.

Instead of replying, he opened a compartment under the control panel of the aircraft and took out a small container.

"What's this?" I asked when he offered it to me.

Lifting the lid, I found two round Voranian pastries I often had for breakfast. Their texture still reminded me of clay. However, the mildly sweet taste had been growing on me.

"You haven't eaten much for breakfast this morning," the Colonel said at my questioning stare. "You tend to get irritated faster when you're hungry."

"Are you about to irritate me, then?" I took out one of the two disks.

He was right, in the rush of this morning, I'd left most of my breakfast untouched. However, I hadn't expected him to notice or, even less so, to pack a snack for me.

"Thanks." I took a big bite off the pastry. "So, can I go shopping?"

"On your own? Under no circumstances."

As he had predicted, irritation stirred in me. I took it out on the pastry in my hand, chomping off another huge chunk of it before replying.

"Why not? It's not dangerous. It's not like we're in a war zone or something. Voran is a civilized city."

"Except that you'd stand out from the crowd wherever you go." His expression turned to stone, unyielding.

I knew I'd attract a lot of attention, but that didn't mean I'd be attacked or whatever it was that the Colonel was afraid of.

From everything I'd learned about Voran, it was a peaceful place. Its people didn't get into fights for no reason, and I certainly wasn't planning to give anyone any reason to attack me.

"I'm used to the unwanted attention, by now," I assured him. "Stares and whispers don't bother me much."

"I'm afraid someone may do something more than that," he replied grimly.

"Like what? Kidnap me for ransom?"

"Maybe."

"Does it happen often in this city?"

"No."

"Well, then how likely is that to happen to me?"

"I don't know!" He raised his voice, after all. "But I don't want to take chances to find out. Besides, you don't know the city that well, or the mall layout."

"Really?" I groaned, unable to hold the frustration at bay any longer. "Come on, I'm sure I'll be able to find my way around a mall. Besides, I would like to see more of Voran. Part of the reason why I came to Neron was to learn a new culture, and I can't learn much about the city just by flying over it."

He drew in some air, and I braced myself for another argument.

"Fine," he conceded, so suddenly, I thought I hadn't heard him right. "Let me think about it. I may come up with something."

Well, it went better than I'd expected, this time. Deprived of a reason to argue, I silently ate my pastry.

Maybe it was possible for us to find some middle ground on other things, too? Eventually?

Chapter 13

THE DAY AFTER MY FIRST full week of classes, the Colonel happened to have a morning off. An early meeting of his had been cancelled, and he wasn't going to work until later.

We had breakfast together. Then he went downstairs to the exercising room for a workout, and I decided to help Omni plant the gray-blue flowers, *lilcae*, that the Colonel wanted in the dining room.

"These are rather modest, compared to the others you have in here." I set the tray with the dirt pellets containing the delicate plants on the dining table that Omni had covered with a sheet of plastic. "Why would Colonel order them?"

"He hasn't shared the reason."

"Well, that doesn't surprise me. He doesn't explain his actions very often, does he?" Climbing on the table, I lifted a pellet to place it into the cluster of tubular planters that were a part of the chandelier.

One of Omni's drones hovered over my shoulder. "Make sure you cover the tip of the bottom leaf with dirt, too. It'll sprout roots and will make for a more sophisticated root system." The AI was a huge stickler for rules, following the gardening processes from the planet Aldrai to a T.

I did as instructed, carefully tucking the tip of the pale-green leaf into the dirt.

"Interesting," Omni's voice sounded from his frame by the table, this time.

I glanced that way. The image of my face, with the freshly planted flower next to it, appeared on the screen. Two circles zoomed in, one on my eye, the other one on the little flower of the plant.

"The color of *lilcae* flowers is nearly identical to the color of your eyes. I wonder if that was why the Colonel wanted them here."

I snorted a laugh, gently patting the dirt around the pellet with the seedling I'd just inserted into the planter.

"That's definitely not the reason why he ordered them. The Colonel doesn't give a shit about my eyes."

"Madam Kyradus, such language is unbecoming of a lady," Omni scolded.

"Well, it's a good thing I'm not a *lady*, then," I laughed.

"You are the wife of one of the top officials in the country—"

"The *top official* also swears like a blacksmith, in case you haven't noticed. And don't you tell me it's fine because he is a male."

"There certainly is a clear divide between gender expectations for men and women in Voran—"

"Okay, okay." I waved him. "I'm not going to argue with you about the socially acceptable gender roles around here. I'm not defying Voranian culture. I didn't come here to start a cultural revolution. But if I let one or two naughty words slip in private, no one is going to be worse off because of it, are they? The Colonel doesn't mind it anymore." He'd stopped commenting on my occasional swearing long ago. "And you wouldn't tell anyone anyway, would you?" I wiggled my eyebrows at the frame.

The image on his screen scrambled, then a beeping sound came.

"What's that? Omni, are you okay?"

"Incoming aircraft," he informed me.

"Where?" I hopped off the table. "Why?"

During the weeks I'd spent in the Colonel's house, we hadn't had any visitors.

"What do they want?" I brushed dirt off my hands.

"The reason for the visit has not been shared with me."

"What *has* been shared? Did the Colonel say anything? Is he expecting someone?"

"There are no visitors on his schedule for today."

"What should I do?" I took off the frilly bib apron I wore to keep dirt off my yellow dress with a poofy skirt trimmed with white lace. "Do I just let them in? Play hostess?" What if they were high officials to see the Colonel? I'd surely mess up some protocol while receiving them. "I should get the Colonel."

I dashed toward the side stairs leading down to the exercise room on the lower level.

"Who could they be?" I muttered under my breath on the way to the stairs.

"The cousin of Colonel Kyradus," Omni suddenly informed me. "Madam Lievoa Kyradus."

As an unmarried woman, Lievoa still went by her first name and the last name of her father, the brother of the Colonel's dad.

"Omni!" I stopped in my tracks before reaching the stairs. "Why didn't you say that right away?"

"You haven't asked until now."

I huffed a frustrated breath, turning to go to the parking platform.

"With all the technology you're packing in that frame of yours, one would think you should be able to announce the visitors by name before I completely lose my mind here."

"Daisy!" Lievoa jumped out of her small, metallic-pink aircraft and ran to me as I entered the parking platform.

"Hi Lievoa." I smiled, bracing myself for her greeting and already feeling sorry for my ears.

She grabbed on to them, pulling me in for a smooch.

"So nice to see you again! Ready to go?"

"Go? Where?" I stared at her in confusion.

Letting go of my ears, Levoa straightened her pink dress printed with purple flower garlands. Her horns, hooves, and the tip of her tail were painted with thin, silver spirals.

"To the mall. Grevar said you wanted to go shopping." She chatted so energetically, the strings of multicolored beads and painted shells that were draped over her chest rattled. "We can spend the whole day together, have lunch at the mall, too. I'll just need to stop at my dress shop for a little while, and I have a polishing appointment this afternoon."

"What? Hold on." I waved both hands at her, feeling rather confused. "When did he speak with you? He hasn't said anything to me. It's the spice market I wanted to go to. Omni?" I called back into the main room. "Did the Colonel add any appointments to the schedule for me today."

"No. Madam Kyradus," came the calm voice of the AI.

"The spice market is adjacent to the Central Mall," Lievoa spoke a little slower, probably to give me some time to catch up. "Grevar called me a couple of days ago, asking me to take you shopping because he didn't want you to go alone. I said I'd have to look at my schedule, my days are pretty busy, you know."

She rubbed her chin, pausing for a moment.

"Well, come to think of it, I don't believe I ever got back to him to confirm." She shrugged. "Anyway. I happen to have some time today. And here I am. Do you want to come or not?"

"Oh, I do! Give me a moment, I'll be ready in no time." I pivoted on my heels to run up to the bedroom, then turned back to her. "Do I need to change? What do you think?"

Lievoa gave me a critical once-over. "No. This dress is lovely. One of my favorites. You may just want to add some jewelry, it looks kind of bare otherwise."

"Okay, come wait in the main room." I waved her to follow me inside. "Would you like some tea in the meantime? Maybe?"

"No. We'll eat at the mall. Hurry up, please. I'm a very busy woman and have places to be."

Leaving her in the main room, I ran upstairs. In the closet, I changed from my comfy ballet flats into a pair of dressier closed-toe sandals. Roaming through the box of jewelry I had brought with me, I searched for something more appropriate for Neron.

My thin silver chains and fresh-water pearls seemed way too understated for this planet. And I didn't dare wear the jewelry set that the Colonel had given to me—his priceless family heirloom—to the mall.

Finally, I pulled out a long string of large, bright glass beads I thought were pretty but too big and loud to wear to most places on Earth. In Voran, these should do just fine.

I wound the string of beads around my neck a few times then ran downstairs.

"I'll let the Colonel know I'm leaving!" I shouted to Lievoa on my way to the stairs leading to the exercise room on the lower level.

The invigorating scent of heat and male—the Colonel's scent—reached me even before I'd made it to the last step.

He was training in the middle of the room, sparring with one of the stuffed electronic dummies.

Dressed in nothing but a pair of tight shorts, the Colonel attacked the dummy while gracefully evading its maneuvers. Not restricted by his stiff uniform, his movements were both smooth and powerful. His fur, slick with sweat, was plastered to his bulging muscles underneath.

I stared at him, mesmerized by this blatant display of masculinity. Whether anyone thought the Colonel handsome or not, no one would deny his inescapable animalistic appeal. My body had responded to it from the very first moment we'd met. Knowing him so much better now had only weakened my defenses against it.

I was no longer afraid of his raw power; I craved to feel it in other ways. I imagined those arms wrapped around me in a crushing embrace, his mouth devouring mine with abandon. Those trim hips of his fitted perfectly between my thighs... I wanted him to take me with the same passion he put into the fight.

Since that first night when he fiercely tried to claim me as his wife, there hadn't been anything physical between us, save for an occasional hand-holding. And now, I was afraid there never would be. The thought filled me with a deep sense of loss.

His tail swaying back for balance, the Colonel crouched down, evading yet another strike from the dummy. He then kicked his hoof out, landing it in the robot's side.

A holographic display flickered to life over the dummy's head, its impassive voice read aloud the score of the strength and number of hits.

Yanking out the towel stuffed into a pocket on the dummy, the Colonel wiped the sweat from his face and neck. As he turned, he saw me.

"Daisy?" He walked over to me, and I suddenly forgot how to breathe.

Up close, his presence was even more overwhelming, overloading all my senses. His hot, intoxicating scent wrapped around me like a caress. The sight of him—tall, broad, and strong—filled my vision. The fur on his belly was much shorter than on his arms and chest, making his granite abs appear as if they were covered in fine velvet.

I clenched my hands into fists at my sides, fighting the intense desire to reach out and stroke him.

"...something happened?"

I realized suddenly that the Colonel was talking to me while I ogled the hell out of him.

"Sorry..." I blinked, trying to remember what I came here for.

"Are you okay?" he asked with concern, making me feel dumb.

The tell-all blush instantly heated my cheeks.

"No... I mean yes. I'm fine." I tore my gaze from his hips and abs with an effort, focusing it on the room behind him instead. "Sorry...um, Lievoa is here."

"Lievoa? She never got back to me." He tossed the towel back to the dummy.

"She forgot." My gaze returned to him again, drawn to his body like a magnet. I stared at his wide chest covered in gray, wavy fur. "She has the time to take me shopping right now."

"When will you be back?" He stepped closer. So close, the heat radiating from him brushed against my bare arms.

"Later this afternoon." I knew I should take a step back, to keep the distance, but I stayed, stealing another moment of being this intimately close to him.

"Will she feed you lunch, then?" he asked as if I were a kid going to someone's house for a playdate.

I couldn't hold back a smile at the comparison.

"We'll eat at the mall."

"Omni," the Colonel tossed over his shoulder to a drone hovering nearby. "Do you have a credit bracelet for Daisy?"

Another drone silently floated down the stairs with a wide, golden bangle grasped in one of its pincers.

"Buy whatever you want." The Colonel clipped the bangle around my left wrist, letting his fingers linger on my arm for a few moments. "And be careful out there."

"Thank you."

"Take your tablet with you, call me right away if you need any help."

I nodded with a warm feeling of gratitude spreading through me. It felt awfully nice to have someone like the Colonel just a call away, ready to rush to me if I needed help.

"YOU ABSOLUTELY SHOULD get this!" Lievoa straightened out the voluminous skirt of the chiffon cocktail dress I was trying on in her shop. "This pale-green color goes so well with your hair."

"I've already spent a lot of the Colonel's money," I argued.

We'd shopped for over an hour in the spice market, talking to dozens of vendors. Each of them had some advice for the Earth girl who was into baking. I had taken a lot of notes and bought a bunch of stuff that we'd sent to Lievoa's aircraft by mall drones.

"Why do you call him the Colonel?" she asked, unexpectedly. "Close family members normally refer to each other by their first names. And husband and wife are as close as it gets."

"Oh. It's...um, it's an Earth thing," I said quickly, frantically searching for another topic. "Can I see that scarf, please?"

Lievoa's dress shop turned out to be a huge, multi-level store, with drones in every corner and live shopping assistants on every floor. Lievoa had talked me into trying on a few dresses. I couldn't say no. The clothes were gorgeous, and I'd always loved playing dress-up. I'd had no intention of buying any, though.

"This one?" She tied a gold scarf around my head in leu of a headband. "It's perfect! You have to get it, too. I'll give you a family discount, of course, and don't worry about spending Grevar's money. What did he say when he gave you this credit bracelet?"

"Buy whatever you want."

"See?" She shrugged casually. "This is a woman's bangle, he obviously had it made specifically for you. It's every man's dream to have a wife he can dote on. Grevar will be glad you had fun and found something you liked. Just say 'thank you' to him when you wear your new clothes for the first time. It will make him happy."

Except that I wasn't the Colonel's wife. Not in the true sense of that word. My parenting course was ending in two weeks. After that, Olvar and Zun would be regularly spending two days a week at home. I felt like I was finally about to fulfill my true purpose for being here. My actual employment was about to start.

Would an employer splurge on his nanny like that? Even if she was disguised as his wife?

Would a real nanny have the intense desire to rub her hands all over her boss's abs the way I had this morning?

The role of a nanny came with the restrictions I was beginning to realize I couldn't follow. That's where all this confusion was coming from in the first place. My head, my body—and yes, my heart, too—were all in disagreement on what I should and shouldn't want.

I closed my eyes for a moment, struggling to collect my thoughts and emotions.

A nanny would negotiate for a salary to be paid to her, instead of buying a dress. Money defined a relationship better than words.

A wife would buy the clothes without overthinking it.

Which one did I really want to be?

"I'll take it," I said to Lievoa.

"Great! Let me find some matching shoes, too. We'll need to custom order those, you know, with your feet being the only pair of human feet in all of Voran." She giggled, grabbing her tablet.

After buying the dress, the scarf, the shoes, and also a few pieces of fashion jewelry to go with all of it, I finally managed to leave the store.

Lievoa and I had lunch under one of the indoor gazebos draped in flower garlands in the mall. Then, we went to the beauty boutique where Lievoa had a polishing appointment booked that afternoon. "Polishing," as she had explained to me on the way, included a series of procedures meant to make her horns, hooves, and claws smooth and shiny. The service also included painting designs on them.

Unlike many other places in Voran, there was almost the same number of women as men in the Central Mall. No one appeared to be in a hurry. Groups of people gathered under vine-draped gazebos built between the stores, enjoying refreshments served by drones and chatting with friends.

As expected, I got a lot of stares. By now, news of my arrival had been broadcast everywhere. The pictures of me on the Colonel's arm at the Governor's Ball had been in every print publication and online tabloid.

Most people knew who I was, but it didn't stop them from eyeing me with curiosity. Those who knew Lievoa approached us to say hi to her and to take a closer look at me, which considerably slowed our progress through the mall.

"Listen," Lievoa said to me as we came to the beauty boutique. "You have no horns or hooves to polish. This will be boring for you."

"Oh, it's okay. I don't mind waiting."

"It'll take at least an hour. Too long to wait with nothing to do." She glanced around. "I can't really send you store browsing on your own, either."

"I can take care of myself," I protested.

"Oh, I don't doubt that, but Grevar would lift me on his horns if he learned I left you alone in the middle of the crowded mall. Here!" She dragged me to a tall arch of pale pink flowers that marked the entrance to a store with a glowing sign over it.

An AI frame that looked like a festive version of Omni, draped in sheer, shimmering fabrics and decorated with paint and flowers, rolled out to greet us.

"Welcome to the Dream Spa," it said in a melodious, feminine voice.

"Hi," Lievoa yanked me to her by my hand. "A massage for the lady, please?"

"Would it be for excitement or relaxation?" the frame enquired.

"Relaxation. How long does a full body massage take?"

"An hour."

"Perfect." Lievoa turned to me. "You'll have a massage while I get my stuff done. By the time you're ready, I'll be here to get you."

She bounced off, leaving me in the care of the AI.

The frame led me into a changing room. The walls here were covered in the same shimmering pink material and flowers.

"Please change here." The arrow on the screen pointed at the cream-coloured silk robe on the wall. "And leave your clothing in this room."

As soon as the AI left me alone and the door to the dressing room closed, I got out of my dress and shoes. I found no spa slippers anywhere, as was to be expected. Wrapped into the bathrobe, I padded out of the room barefoot.

"I'm ready," I said to the frame. "Now what?"

"Excellent!" the AI exclaimed in an excited tone. "Follow me to the machine, please."

It took me to a larger room this time.

A curious contraption in gold-tone metal and black glass stood in the middle. Shaped like a long cylinder, it vaguely reminded me of tanning beds back on Earth. Except that unlike a tanning bed, this cylinder was completely closed, like a capsule.

"Is that how you get a massage on Neron?" I asked, wondering how exactly this worked.

"Yes. It has been programmed for an hour for you, but you will be able to adjust the settings as you go. The machine is very intuitive. It uses your own past experiences to design the best custom program for you."

"Sounds exciting."

"Enjoy." The AI rolled out of the room, and the sliding door closed behind it.

The lid of the cylindrical machine in front of me silently opened, revealing a padded interior. It appeared cozy like a cocoon, with round, gold-framed openings in seemingly random locations on the sides of the capsule and inside the lid.

I stroked the gray-velvet-padded surface, suddenly thinking about the Colonel's abs again.

It would be a long year living side by side with a man who had this effect on me. However, leaving him was the last thing I wanted to do, now.

My physical attraction to him was in no way criminal or forbidden. The Colonel was my husband, dammit. The whole of Voran already thought we were having sex as much and as often as we wanted.

The problem was, he didn't seem to want me in that way, anymore.

"Once was enough for me," he'd said when talking about Shula rejecting his marriage proposal.

Proud man that he was, I feared he would never forget my initial rejection, either. I didn't regret my behaviour that first night. The timing had been wrong, and we didn't know each other at all. Now, however, if the Colonel made another move on me, I wouldn't reject him.

By now, I got to know him enough to appreciate and respect him as a person. He was a strong and reliable man like a rock, with a gentle side to him that made my insides melt. I wanted him. In every sense.

Had he so much as touched me in his home gym this morning, I wouldn't be standing here, alone and sexually frustrated.

"Sooner or later you will want to be fucked by a man. Then, you'll beg me for it."

His words sounded prophetic now. This time, even the idea of begging didn't seem that appalling.

"And it could only be me."

Well, I didn't want anyone else.

I sighed deeply. The gesture made my nipples rub against the smooth silk of the robe. Sparks of desire fluttered from my chest down to my thighs. The smooth caress of the silk robe against my skin only made it worse.

I ripped the bathrobe off, then climbed into the massage machine.

"Welcome," a soothing voice flowed over me as the lid lowered down smoothly the moment I'd lain down. "Please close your eyes and focus on the vision of your mind."

The vision of my mind?

Whatever the heck did that mean?

I did what I was told, though, closing my eyes. With the light inside the capsule dimmed, I could hardly see anything, anyway.

A cool strip of metal pressed to my forehead, circling my head. I jerked at the contact.

"Nothing to worry about here," the voice reassured me as soothing music started to play in the background. "You are safe and calm."

Calm? I wasn't so sure about that.

A fine mist covered my skin with warm fragrant oil then a series of soft rubbery things rolled up and down my body, massaging every muscle under my skin.

"This is really nice," I murmured.

"Please select a setting."

A slideshow of images went through my mind. My bedroom in my parents' house when I was little. A white-sand beach we had gone to while on vacation. A large rock in the valley behind my Grandma's old house. The luxurious, round bed that used to be Colonel's but was mine for the next ten and a half months.

"That one," I whispered.

The picture no longer was in front of me, but around me. The machine seemed to have disappeared, as I lay on the bed in the Colonel's bedroom, the starry night sky over the flowery canopy twinkling above me.

As the things massaged and rubbed my body, my thoughts went to the Colonel once again. The illusion of being in his house was so real, I started wondering where under the glass domes would he be while I lay on his bed, naked. Would he be reading the news downstairs? Or working on his tablet? Or maybe training in his exercise room again? Hot and sweaty in his barely decent shorts...

"May we suggest a change in the program?" the machine's voice filtered through.

My mind still floated somewhere, focusing wasn't easy. "Okay."

"A relaxation mode has been requested. However, our sensors indicate that the excitement mode would be more beneficial for you, right now."

"Excitement?"

"Would you prefer one partner or multiple for this session?"

"An *exciting* massage partner, you mean? I'm afraid I don't get—"

"You don't need to answer any questions vocally," the voice continued, soothing and pleasant. "Let your mind make the selection."

Another series of images floated through my mind like a slideshow.

The face of my grandma's hot neighbour I had a crush on when still in high school. A couple of my ex-boyfriends. Several male celebrities from Earth—two movie actors, a male model, and a few Olympic athletes.

Then, the face of the Colonel filled my mind's vision. The usual grumpy expression in his hard-set mouth. The eerie red eyes under his long, thick eyelashes.

My heart skipped a beat at the sight of him. I believed I could even smell his heady scent again, his large, hard body radiating heat and energy after a vigorous work-out.

Unlike the rest of the images, his didn't disappear. His face just moved a little farther, letting his muscular torso come into view. The Colonel was standing on his knees over me, straddling my thighs as I lay in his bed. I could even feel the weight of him, pressing me down.

And he was naked.

Completely.

"Oh, no..." Air rushed out of my chest as he leaned closer.

"Yesss," he hissed. The tip of his impossibly long tongue trailed along the side of my neck.

A tide of warmth came over me, flooding me with pleasure and taking my breath away. The feelings I'd been suppressing rushed to the surface.

His large hands palmed my breasts, warm and rough against my skin. He rubbed my nipples with his thumbs, then squished my breasts together, burying his face between them.

Something nudged between my thighs—his tail, I realized, squirming under him.

Turning his head, he sucked one of my nipples into his mouth, while the pointy end of the arrowhead of his tail slid inside me.

"Oh God..." I moaned, and he grunted in reply, switching to my other nipple, sucking it in and swirling that long deft tongue of his over it.

The point of his tail twirled just inside my opening, tugging at my most sensitive spot that felt hot and swollen.

"Please, please, fuck me," I begged, with pitiful needy sounds in my throat.

With a growl, he flipped me onto my belly then yanked my hips up, fitting himself behind me. An incredibly large, hot cock pushed inside me, stretching me around it.

"Oh yes..." I whimpered. "I need this, so much."

His hand in my hair, his other arm around my hips to hold me in place for him, he shoved his entire length in, in one thrust.

I screamed out in pleasure, my knees shaking from need.

He yanked my head back, the sting from the roots of my hair spread with shivers through the rest of my body.

I fisted my hands in the sheets, trying not to fly off the bed as he pounded hard into me from behind. Each shove of his cock into me came with a slam of his flesh against mine, my swollen nipples dragging along the bedding with an added tantalising sensation.

"Yes, yes, please..." I chanted, as the tip of his tail relentlessly flicked between my legs, taking me higher and higher.

Hot lust crested in a swell. Then, the orgasm slammed into me, hard and furious. Pleasure exploded through me, making my limbs shake.

"Oh God, I can't take it..." I buried my face in the bedding as waves of ecstasy rolled through me. Again and again.

"We hope you have found your experience with Dream Spa satisfactory," a voice filtered through from somewhere—from another dimension, it seemed. "All referrals are highly appreciated."

The sensation of the magnificent dick inside me had disappeared. Curled on my side, I was lying inside the pleasure capsule, the luxurious padding soaking in my sweat and the remnants of my arousal.

I'd just had the best sex in my life.

And it all had been mostly in my head.

"WAS IT GOOD?" LIEVOA greeted me when I finally made it out of the spa, fully dressed but on the shaking legs.

All I could do was just nod in reply.

She fixed my hair and adjusted my skirt for me.

"You look like you've just been ravaged by a wild beast," she fussed.

She had no idea...

Chapter 14

GREVAR

With the boys coming home that weekend, Daisy appeared to be growing increasingly more anxious.

She had cleaned and decorated the twins' room, insisting on doing most of the work herself and refusing his or Omni's help. Even when everything was done and ready for them, she continued to act differently than before.

She'd been unusually quiet at mealtimes, going upstairs right after dinner. He knew she stayed up late, as he heard her moving about the bedroom until past his bedtime. Yet she wouldn't stay downstairs with him, as if avoiding him on purpose.

He missed their time together.

He'd been trying to muster some patience to keep his hands off her since that one disastrous attempt at the beginning. Instead, he'd been learning to enjoy his new wife in other ways. There was so much more to being with a woman than just sex, he'd discovered.

Before her visit to the mall, he believed they'd been making a good progress. He loved coming home to her after a long day at work. Their conversations had grown longer, their arguments rare and far between. She'd agreed to stay for an entire year, and he'd even begun to hope that theirs might be a true marriage one day.

Now, it felt like there had been a setback, but he couldn't figure out why.

Daisy had been talking about missing her family. He didn't like her leaving the house on her own, but maybe she was getting lonely, staying home every day after her parenting class?

In an attempt to cheer her up, he'd decided to have a dinner party at his house the first evening the boys were home. It would be a very small event, pleasant without being overwhelming.

He'd invited Lievoa. Daisy seemed to be getting along well with her, which pleased him. He didn't always understand his cousin's thought process and disagreed with some of her actions, but Lievoa was family. She had a good heart, and he loved her.

The Governor and Shula had agreed to come for drinks after dinner, just before the boys would go to bed. After her latest delivery, Shula had started the customary recovery process between pregnancies and wasn't leaving the house for long these first few weeks.

Instead of being excited, Daisy appeared even more flustered when he told her about their guests.

In addition to planning the dinner menu with Omni for tonight, she also woke up early in the morning to get everything ready for the desserts she wanted to make, using her recipes from Earth.

The two of them had taken the boys to the Museum of The Natural History of Neron that morning. Zun and Olvar had participated in every interactive exhibit they could find. They ran, climbed, and explored. As a result of all the activities, the twins could barely keep their eyes open in the aircraft on the way home.

As soon as the boys went down for a nap in the afternoon, Daisy dashed back to the kitchen. Despite her earlier claims, baking didn't seem to be relaxing her today. Amazing smells wafted from the kitchen, mixed with clanking dishes and occasional swearing. Unlike Voranian women, she didn't hold back in her choice of words when she was irritated or upset.

"Fuck!" came from the kitchen as he was watching a video on his tablet on the couch in the sitting room. "The *chocolate* isn't really a *chocolate* if it doesn't melt. Is it?"

He had no idea what that meant, but it bothered him that she sounded upset. He liked seeing that happy smile on her face. It reminded him of sunrise in its increasing brightness.

Her dress might've first attracted his attention to her application picture. But it was her sunny smile that had made him feel close to the strange alien woman in the photo before he'd even had a chance to meet her. From the moment he saw Daisy's smile in that picture, he knew he wanted to have her in his life.

"Colonel." Daisy walked into the sitting room, a red polka-dot apron tied over her blue-checkered dress—both dusted with white powder and smeared with pink, brown, and cream. "We're going to have one dessert less today. The mousse turned out a disaster."

He set his tablet aside. Her crestfallen expression made him want to hug her, and the smidge of pink icing he'd just spotted on her nose made him want to lick her...

There were many things he dreamed of doing to her. The effort of doing nothing at all had been the most excruciating.

"How many types of dessert are there going to be this evening?" he asked.

"I've planned five, but it's only going to be four now." She plopped on the couch next to him, raising a cloud of white powder from her skirts. "The freaking thing that I believed would be the closest to the *chocolate* from Earth solidified into a rock instead of melting when heated."

"Isn't there usually just one dessert after dinner? Four sounds like three more than we need," he said evenly. Judging by her flushed cheeks and trembling lips, she was teetering on the verge of a meltdown.

"You don't understand!" She sounded devastated. "I wanted to have a variety for the boys to get a taste of food from Earth." She shifted to face him, her bent knee landing on his thigh. "Don't worry, I'm making tiny-little portions. The boys each can have up to three of those and still stay within the recommended dose of sugar, as per the Ministry's requirements."

"If they can only have three and you've made four types, doesn't it mean that there is still one too many?"

She inhaled quickly, looking ready to argue, then exhaled slowly, as if deflating along with her argument.

"I guess you're right..." She rubbed her chin. "They'll still have some choice even without the stupid mousse." She gazed at him then, tilting her head, her expression more relaxed. "How were you able to stay this calm when I was about to lose it? You, of all people?"

He chuckled, "We both know you've calmly stopped me from blowing up on more than one occasion, too."

"It's a good thing that only one of us tends to freak out at a time, now. There has been much less screaming and yelling lately, don't you think?"

She smiled now, and he exhaled with relief.

The atmosphere in their house had definitely quieted down. At the beginning, they had fanned each other's flames during an argument. By now, however, he'd learned to read Daisy's moods much better and could predict the approaching storm before it happened. He managed to cool her temper flare-ups before they had a chance to blow out of proportions. He'd noticed, she had a similar calming effect on him, too.

Her gaze fell on her leg resting on top of his, and she scooted back quickly, breaking their contact. Her cheeks flushed again, their bright color now rivaled that of her apron.

"Anyway..." She shoved a lock of her hair under the colorful scarf she was wearing to hold back her bright orange tresses. "Four is enough, like you said. I better go change. Lievoa should be here any minute, now."

He watched her go upstairs, his gaze lingering on her quick feet in open sandals as she ran. The sight of her toes no longer shocked him. Nothing about Daisy could ever repulse him. On the contrary, every little thing about her body was extremely appealing. His cock grew painfully hard at the mere thought of how her leg had touched his.

He groaned softly, shifting on the couch to make more space in his pants for his growing erection while he calmed himself down.

Daisy hadn't been her usual bubbly self lately, tripping over her words and blushing violently. Whenever he asked her about it, she acted even more discomfited, denied that anything was wrong, and ran away from him at the earliest opportunity.

Had he done something wrong?

The only other relationship he'd ever had with a woman was with Shula, and it had started and ended in the bedroom. Most interactions outside of the bedroom were new to him.

With Daisy, he proceeded carefully, learning as he went. He worried that she would run all the way back to Earth if he made another mistake. And he already knew he would miss her desperately if that happened.

As happy as he'd been when she'd agreed to stay for the year, a year wasn't enough. He needed her for life. And he had barely over ten months left to figure out how to convince her that he was worth spending a lifetime with.

GREVAR

"Did I miss your dad coming to the city?" Lievoa asked casually, popping a piece of stuffed *esculi* into her mouth. "I thought he had his visit scheduled for like two weeks ago."

"Grandpa is coming?" Olvar immediately picked up on her words.

Zun and Daisy turned to stare at him, too.

"No. He cancelled it."

In fact, Grevar had cancelled it *for* him. Father had been planning to come for a visit with the intension of meeting his new daughter-in-law, of course. Grevar had no doubt his dad would've loved Daisy the moment he met her. Then, if Grevar allowed her to leave him as he'd promised her he would, he'd have to face a severely unpleasant conversation with his father, in addition to everything else he'd be dealing with.

More pressure on him when he already was under a lot of pressure as far as Daisy was concerned—his shoulders ached with the strain. Not to mention the torture that his cock had been enduring ever since she'd moved in. With her around, he'd been in a state of constant arousal, no matter how often he made himself come at night.

"Was your dad planning to visit?" Daisy tilted her head with interest.

"It didn't work out," he muttered quickly. "He had other plans."

"Oh, that's too bad." She gazed at him with those huge eyes of hers, the colour of the *lilcae* flowers.

He had ordered some planted in his office, too. Not because he needed another reminder of Daisy during the day—his thoughts were on her constantly anyway—but because having *lilcae* around somehow made him miss her just a little less. And he did miss her at work—a lot. He even had her application picture framed last week. It was now it on his desk in the office.

What the hell was he supposed to do when she left to go back to Earth?

She couldn't leave. That was the only answer to that question.

"Can we go to grandpa's house, then?" Zun asked.

"No," Grevar bit off, tossing a glare Lievoa's way, annoyed at her for bringing it up.

"What time would be better for him to visit?" Daisy started planning. "Do you think the next weekend would work for him? It'd be great for everyone—the children will be here. And it's Christmas that weekend, which is a big family holiday on Earth. Not that it matters on

Neron, of course…" Her voice trailed off as a shadow moved over her lovely face.

"A holiday?" Zun bounced in his chair.

"Let's do a party!" Olvar slapped his brother's shoulder excitedly.

"Do you have a big party to celebrate *Christmas* back on Earth?" Lievoa asked, with interest.

"Well, mostly just a family dinner." Daisy put down an untouched smocked meat roll, a warm expression shining in her eyes. "Often, the entire family gets together—uncles, aunts, cousins, grandparents. It's a great time to catch up with everyone. People also exchange gifts, eat a lot of desserts, and…well, generally have a good time."

"Oh, it's like the Victory Day?" Olvar shouted in delight. "Right, Dad?"

"Right," he replied flatly. "Minus the military parade and the tribute to the war fallen."

"Well, yeah, but aside from the parade, they're similar," Lievoa argued. "Voranians get together in the outdoor parks and have family picnics, with desserts." She turned to Daisy. "The Victory Day is in the middle of summer, the weather is usually nice and warm, then."

"Christmas is in the winter, when many countries have snow. Like here," Daisy explained.

"I love snow," Zun declared. "Especially building a fort. Can we do it again?"

Olvar snorted a laugh. "You didn't even like fort building."

"I did too!"

"Do you miss home a lot?" Grevar asked Daisy, catching her wistful expression.

"I do," she said, making his heart sink. "But it's not just that. I also miss the Christmas celebrations we used to have when Grandma was still alive. With her, the entire Christmas season was one huge celebration. The two of us would start decorating a month ahead. Every room in her house was decked out with pine branches and ornaments. In the living room, we built an entire Christmas city, with porcelain houses that had real lights inside. Oh, and there was a railroad, with a train that ran on electric rail tracks. It could even whistle."

He watched her face light up as she talked. Propping her head on her hand, Lievoa gazed at Daisy, too, as she spoke. The kids had quieted down, listening to the tales from another world with rapt attention.

"Grandma would take me Christmas shopping, every year," his wife continued. "There was an outdoor market in her town each weekend in December. Even now, whenever I smell hot chocolate I think of those days. We would buy handmade presents for everyone. Then, we would decorate Christmas trees. We always had two, one in her house and one in ours. We would have a dinner at our house on Christmas Eve. Then, my sister and I would stay the night at Grandma's and open all the presents the next morning. Hers were always the most fun. She liked giving people gifts that were personal, but also unique and even whimsical. And of course, it was always a big surprise." Daisy's chest rose with an inhale. "Ever since Grandma passed away, Christmas has never been the same. Still nice, but not the same."

She glanced around the table. He and Lievoa remained quiet. Even the boys appeared subdued.

"Anyway..." Daisy cleared her throat, shrugging her shoulders as if shaking off the lingering sadness of nostalgia for the times long gone. "Dessert time?" She grabbed their empty trays and dashed to the kitchen.

Lievoa followed her with her gaze.

"Human or whatever, Daisy is great," she concluded.

"I like her, too," Zun said firmly. "Daisy is a good friend."

"Well, she is more than a friend, isn't she?" Lievoa turned to the boy. "She is your—"

"Lievoa," Grevar interrupted, putting a warning in his voice.

"I like Daisy," Olvar declared. "And she is staying with us for a whole year!"

"A year?" Lievoa leveled a stare at him. "What are your sons talking about, cousin? Care to explain?"

He cringed inside. He should've foreseen a possibility that his arrangement with Daisy might not remain a secret forever. Maybe, he should've at least considered letting his closest family and friends in on it. Deep inside, however, he'd thought he could fix it somehow. That sooner or later, Daisy would stay with him—for life, not just a year.

"What did you do?" Lievoa frowned, folding her arms across her chest.

"I'm working on it," he muttered.

"I hope you like these!" A tray of desserts in each hand, Daisy rushed in, saving him from a lengthy explanation. Though if he knew his cousin at all, the explanation had just been postponed, not cancelled.

"Tell me what you think about each." Daisy moved around the table, serving the strange looking pieces on individual plates in front of each person at the table. "You only get three," she warned the boys. "But you'll get to choose which ones you want."

Lievoa leaned toward him over the table and hissed into his face, "I like her more than a lot of Voranian women I know. I don't care what you've done, Grevar. Fix it!"

He took a long swig from his glass, nearly choking on his wine.

"Dessert?" Daisy moved to his side with her tray. "Which one would you like?"

She stood so close. Her sweet, flowery scent mixed with the aroma of his wine, more intoxicating than any liquor. Heat radiated from the point where her bare arm touched his shoulder. She bent over holding the tray out for him to make his choice. All he had to do would be to slide his gaze a little sideways to glimpse the tantalizing sight of her breasts inside her neckline...

His cock twitched with ache, and his heart squeezed with longing. Would there ever be an end to this torture? How would he survive if she left?

"Colonel?" she prompted, her voice a bit raspy.

"This one." He pointed at something brown.

He stuffed the whole thing into his mouth the moment she'd set it on his plate. It turned out to be delicious—sweet, with just a hint of bitterness—even though he didn't like sweet foods that much.

"This one is my favorite, I think." Lievoa pointed at the round pastry decorated with a creamy pink flower. "Though, it's really hard to say. They're all so good."

"I like this one, too." Olvar shoved the last of the three pieces on his plate into his mouth.

"Me too." Zun ate all three simultaneously, taking a bite of each at a time. "But I like this one the most." He bit into the round brown thing, the same Grevar just had.

"This is a chocolate cupcake," Daisy cheerfully explained. "Unlike the mousse, I made it with the chocolate equivalent powder. That's why it turned out pretty good. Miss Goodfellow, my old boss at the bakery, used to say that my cupcakes were the best. Her customers always asked for them."

Lievoa clapped her hands. "Daisy, you could get a job in a bakery here, too." She tossed a glare his way.

Did she think Daisy was leaving because he wouldn't let her out of the house on her own? Of course, Lievoa would be accusing him of a million things, right now. But would Daisy getting a job in Voran help him keep her?

"Do people even buy baked goods around here?" Daisy asked. "Everyone has an AI, don't they?"

"They do," Lievoa nodded. "And an AI is great at replicating recipes, but nothing beats the taste of food made by a real person. Bakeries don't release their recipes to the public, either. So, some things can only be bought there and nowhere else. Your parenting course is now over, isn't it?" Lievoa slid him another reproachful glare.

His cousin really seemed to be after his blood now, but she was mistaken. He wasn't against Daisy having a job outside of the house, as long as he could make sure the place was safe. If getting a job would keep Daisy in Voran, he'd do anything to make it happen.

"You could work at the bakery a few mornings a week," Lievoa carried on with her "*Liberating Daisy*" campaign, "and be with the kids on the weekend. There is a very good bakery at the Eastern Mall. The owner, Scurad, is a really nice guy. I can talk to him if you like. I'm sure he'd love to add some *Earth flavor* to his baked goods." She giggled, wiggling her eyebrows.

"No." Grevar shook his head before Daisy had a chance to reply. The idea of her spending any time in a company of another male, even if on a strictly professional level, made the fur on his back rise with ire. "Eastern Mall is on the other side of town," he explained when both women stared at him. "It's too far."

Lievoa narrowed her eyes at him suspiciously.

"Or you could always open your own bakery," she said to Daisy, without taking her stare off him. "It'll give you some freedom and independence to fully enjoy life in Voran."

Chapter 15

WHEN EVERYONE WAS DONE with their dessert, the Colonel, Lievoa, the children, and I moved to the large sitting area in the main room.

The sunset had drawn a glowing haze of red and orange over the sky. Omni kept the lighting in the room on low, which created a soft, cozy atmosphere.

I glanced at Omni's screen nearby. "Time to go to bed soon, boys."

"But we're waiting for more guests!" both objected in unison.

"Governor of Voran, Ashir Kaeya Drustan, and Madam Governor," Omni announced at that moment, with a formal flare in his voice.

My stomach dropped at the sound of Shula's name, as it did when the Colonel had first told me she and her husband would be coming over after dinner tonight.

Shula had made it clear she hated me. She'd also given me some good reasons to dislike her back. The Colonel considered her and her husband his dear friends, however, and I had no choice but to be civil and tolerate her presence. Hopefully, since everyone would be in earshot this time, she wouldn't try to insult me again.

The doors to the parking platform slid open, and the first couple of Voran walked in.

The Governor was dressed in a lime-green suit that highlighted his lemon-yellow eyes. His wife wore a floor-length gown in shimmering gold. It was just as opulent as the purple-green one she'd had on at the ball. No longer pregnant after the delivery of the senator's triplets, she was slimmer and even appeared taller somehow.

"Uncle Ashir! Aunt Shula!" the twins bounced over to them.

Apparently, they were more than just the Colonel's friends. The children obviously considered the Governor and his wife their family.

"Ahh, there you are, little rascals!" The Governor grabbed each of the boys, one by one, tossing them up into the air in greeting.

"Hello, hello, my darlings," Shula cooed, ruffling the fur on their heads. Bending over, she placed a kiss on the forehead of each. "How do you like being home more often now?"

"It's fun!" Olvar twisted out of her arms to hop around with his brother, their tiny hooves beating a staccato rhythm against the tiled floor.

"Dad and Daisy took us to a museum today," Zun announced. "And next weekend, we're going to the Zoo."

Shula slid her gaze my way. For a moment, my heart froze. What would be the appropriate way for the kids to address me if I was indeed their stepmom and their father's wife? I cursed at myself for not verifying this earlier. Would she see through the lie that the Colonel and I had created around his family life? I felt like a fraud.

Despite currently living a lie, I was generally not in the habit of lying. Sooner or later, lies had the tendency to catch up with you, and I wasn't a good enough actress to maintain a fictional story for long, not even for the best of reasons. By now, all this pretending had really begun to wear me out.

The Colonel gave each of his new guests a brief hug then offered them a drink.

"So, Madam Colonel," the Governor addressed me as the drones brought the drinks and we all took our seats. "How do you find living in Voran now? We haven't spoken for a while. Do you still search for similarities in our cultures?"

"The similarities definitely help, but so does learning about the differences. The more I learn the easier it gets." I smiled.

"I suspect your easy disposition and accepting nature are the key here." He swirled his drink in his glass, crossing his right hoof over his left leg. "We all know Kyradus is not an easy one to get along with."

"Oh, no, he is..." I started to defend the Colonel who was sitting next to me on the couch. Turning his way, I saw that he was smiling, not at all offended by the Governor's words. Long-time friends, they obviously knew each other well. I didn't need to defend him, but I said it anyway, "He isn't difficult to get along with at all, once you get to know him. Everyone knows that he is brave, loyal, and strong, but he is also kind, protective, and caring."

I dropped my gaze down, and the Colonel took my hand in his. I squeezed his fingers, grateful for the sense of support I always got from this gesture of his.

Zun plopped on the couch on the other side of me. I noticed that Olvar leaned against Lievoa's legs while sitting on the floor in front of her, his eyelids drooping. We'd all had a long busy day. Despite their nap today, the kids were getting tired.

I glanced at the Colonel then addressed the rest of the room.

"If you don't mind, I'll take the children upstairs. It's their bed time."

I felt Shula's gaze on me as I gathered the kids. Her attention weighed down my shoulders like a pair of bricks.

Escaping to the boys' room allowed me to catch my breath a little. The routine of putting them to bed wasn't new, I studied it in detail during my course. Once Zun and Olvar had calmed down after the excitement of the day, they didn't put up a fight, allowing me to take them through all the steps as per their schedule.

After tucking them into their beds and kissing them goodnight—which was actually one of the steps in their routine, too, though I would have kissed them goodnight even if it wasn't—I drew in a long breath and left their bedroom to go back downstairs.

"Oh, come on, Shula!" Lievoa's agitated voice reached me from below as I descended. "Even *I* know you don't care about the program."

"I supported it," Shula's tone was strained.

"For show!" Lievoa huffed. "Because you knew it was popular with the majority of the population and it made your husband look good. But you've done nothing to make women from Earth feel welcome here. Daisy got hardly any information on life in Voran. It's like you set her up for failure. And Grevar here wouldn't even let his wife out of the house because he's afraid she may get harassed in public."

"I'm not—" the Colonel started.

But Lievoa was on a roll, she pivoted to him before he had a chance to finish, "Do you know what Shula really thinks about the human women who are to come here to marry our men? Do you know what she called Daisy?"

"Lievoa!" Shula's voice rose with warning.

I hurried down the stairs, rushing to stop whatever was about to happen there.

"A sex doll!" Lievoa exclaimed, pointing at me the moment I set my foot in the room.

I froze in place.

Shula sucked in a breath.

Her husband blinked, moving his gaze from me to her then back again.

The Colonel rose from his seat—menacingly slow.

"You are forgetting yourself, Lievoa," he growled.

"Not me!" His fearless cousin leaped up from her chair, too, meeting him face to face. Well, *face to chest* would be more appropriate, since she was so much shorter than him. "That's right. According to Shula, sex is the only thing a human wife is good for to her Voranian husband."

"Oh God." I covered my eyes with my hand.

As much as I'd love to hold Shula accountable for her words, I never wanted to involve the Colonel in this. This was between Shula and me, and I believed I'd already handled it just fine back at the ball. Lievoa had appeared to be satisfied with my response back then, too. I suspected the couple of glasses of wine she'd had this evening might've made her especially vengeful and feisty.

Or maybe something else had set her off?

"Is that true?" the Colonel's voice thundered, prompting me to open my eyes quickly.

He towered over Shula, now. The terrifying expression I hadn't seen for so long was distorting his handsome features.

"Grevar..." Shula squeaked.

"Kyradus!" The Governor finally jumped to his hooves, too. "It's my wife you're talking to!"

"She insulted *my* wife," the Colonel gritted through his teeth. "And I demand an immediate apology."

The atmosphere in the room grew thick with tension, which I couldn't bear.

"Colonel..." I took a step his way.

Suddenly, Shula lifted her hand up in a call to silence.

"I apologize," she said loud and clear, slowly rising from her chair. "I voiced some rushed conclusions out of concern for my close friend, and I regret it deeply."

I'd never seen an apology delivered in such a dignified fashion. Shula wasn't born as Madam Governor, but she'd sure grown into her position nicely. She wore it with ease and style.

As well as it was done, however, her apology brought more questions, I imagined, than it had answered.

The Colonel's frown grew deeper. "What exactly are you talking about?"

"I'm regretting and retracting the words I said to your wife that day. By insulting her, I've insulted you. Please accept my apologies."

"It's Daisy you should be apologising to," Lievoa noted grimly.

"Daisy," Shula pivoted my way. "May I have a minute of your time, please? In private?"

Oh, boy. The last thing I wanted was a one-on-one talk with Shula. Did she have more insults to toss in my face when no one was around but me?

The Colonel stepped to my side and took my hand in his.

"Say it here, in my presence." He lowered his horns her way.

She glanced at our linked hands then stared back at me.

"Please," she added insistently.

I believed I heard sincerity in her voice. What harm could there be in hearing her out? I could simply leave if I didn't like what she had to say. Here, in the Colonel's house, I certainly felt more at home than at the Governor's Palace.

"Okay. We can talk in the sitting room off the kitchen." I patted the back of the Colonel's hand soothingly. "I'll be right back," I promised.

"WOULD YOU LIKE TO SIT down?" I gestured awkwardly at one of several comfy armchairs in the small sitting area.

Shula shook her head in response, the glowing light of the room twinkling along the golden swirls painted on her horns. Taking a sip of wine from the tall glass in her hand, she remained standing.

Surrounded by the long planters with tall lattices of vines and flowers, this wasn't even a separate room, just a space between the Colonel's kitchen and the enclosed breakfast patio.

The planters here had elaborate waterfall features. The soothing sound of trickling water muffled our voices. The distance of this space from the main area and from everyone else also ensured that our conversation remained private—as Shula had requested. I only hoped I would not come to regret humoring her on that.

"I accept your apology," I said tentatively. "If that's what you wanted to talk about."

She lowered her wine glass, pinning me with her stare.

"Believe it or not, I mean it. I'm sorry for talking to you the way I did that day."

"Okay."

"It's true. I had my reservations about the program. I even urged Ashir not to move ahead with it, despite the generally favorable response to it from the public."

"When did your 'opposition' to it start?" I crossed my arms on my chest. "Let me guess. When my husband was chosen as the first man to get a human wife?"

She darted a sharp gaze my way.

I released a long breath and lowered myself into one of the chairs, not caring whether I was breaking any protocols by sitting in her presence while she was standing.

"You rejected him years ago," I said. "You married another man, but you wanted the Colonel to stay single. Why? So he'd be there for you in case you ever changed your mind?"

"I'm not..." She lifted her hand, shaking her head. "I was never thinking about *changing my mind,* Daisy. I do not regret my decision to marry Ashir."

"Why, then? Why do you hate the idea of the Colonel and I being together?"

"I don't *hate* it." She brushed aside a voluminous curl of her fur that had fallen over her forehead.

Huffing a breath, she plopped into the chair next to mine abruptly, in a not so dignified fashion this time.

"To be completely honest," she said, "I might've had some personal, selfish reasons to oppose this. Grevar and I have a history. We used to be lovers..." She glanced my way. "He told you that, didn't he?"

I nodded grimly.

"That ended when I accepted Ashir's proposal over Grevar's. However, even after my marriage, as Grevar's friend, I remained the most important woman in his life. The idea of being replaced by someone else in that role was hard to accept at the beginning."

"Well, that's just..." I inhaled deeply, momentarily lost for words.

"I know. I said it was selfish." She waved a hand. "You see, as a friend, I care about him maybe even more than when we were a couple. And when I first saw you... I didn't believe you cared about him nearly as much."

I moved to protest, but she stopped me with another hand gesture.

"You showed up at the ball, dressed in the latest fashion Grevar had paid for, sporting his treasured family jewelry, and showing no understanding of what you've got and no appreciation for any of it. At least I saw none. What I saw was a little human gold digger, spewing lies—"

"Okay, you know what, that's enough!" I jumped up from my chair. "You're entitled to your opinion and stuff, but I've no desire to listen to any more insults. And I don't have to. Here, you're in *my* house—"

"Exactly." She smiled unexpectedly, placing her hand on my arm in a calming gesture. "This is your house, your family, and your husband. I have no doubts about any of that now. You care about his children, and I believe the two of you are truly in love. He deserves nothing less."

I blinked at her then plopped back into my chair.

"And you saw all of that in the few minutes since you got here?"

She lifted a well-groomed eyebrow.

"I don't need much longer than that, I know Grevar well enough to spot the difference in him in seconds. He doesn't give affection easily. With him, it has to be earned, and you've obviously done that. And you... I see you're really trying to make him happy, which is commendable. It makes me feel better about this whole thing."

"Well, thanks." I rolled a shoulder back awkwardly, unsure whether to be glad or annoyed by the praise I hadn't asked for from her.

Shula continued meanwhile, "I know you don't consider me a friend—"

"That title has to be earned, too," I snapped.

"Right." She lowered her head in consideration. "And earning it takes time. Meanwhile, I'd ask of you not to shut me out of your family life."

I watched her face for any duplicity, however, her expression appeared sincere.

"Daisy, I know you have the power and probably the desire to close your home to me, after the way I've treated you. I'm asking you not to do that."

"Why?"

"Well, I have no maternal feelings for the children I've given birth to. Babies are immediately taken away from their birth mothers to bond with their fathers. But I'm attached to Grevar's boys. They are the children of one of my closest friends and are like nephews to me. I'm fond of them and enjoy watching them grow. I'd love to remain a part of their lives."

I clasped my hands in my lap, thinking back to the way the boys greeted Shula when she'd arrived tonight. They certainly had some relationship with her, and I'd hate to deprive them of that.

"Okay, fine, let's just keep things the way they are then," I said. "You've said something you shouldn't have, you've apologized for that, and I've accepted it. It's all good now. As long as you treat me and my family with respect, you can remain the family friend that you are. Deal?"

I offered her my hand.

"Deal?" she stared at it confused.

"Yeah, well, let's just shake on it." I took her hand in mine, giving it a brief shake. "This means our verbal agreement is now sealed."

"Interesting." She squeezed my hand in response. "It's a deal, then."

"And while we're at it," I added, releasing her hand. "Putting in place some kind of a welcoming program for the human women coming to Voran is a great idea. Moving planets can be overwhelming at first."

She nodded slowly, with a thoughtful expression on her face.

"I believe the Liaison Committee had a few proposals on that. It might be a good time to look into them." She met my gaze straight on. "I'm not promising to be perfect, Daisy, but I'll do my best to try harder."

Chapter 16

<u>GREVAR</u>

When the guests finally left that night, Daisy wanted to sit on the large enclosed patio off the dining room for a little while.

He realized the party had turned out to be anything but relaxing for her. After she and Shula had returned from their private talk, the atmosphere had thankfully improved. The conversation had flowed much easier. He'd even heard Daisy laugh a few times.

He knew she must be tired, especially after having woken up so early that morning.

"Are you sure you don't want to go to bed right away?" he asked, catching her trying to stifle a yawn.

"Soon." She nodded, taking a seat in an armchair made from *rollu* vine, dried and woven into the shape of a recliner. "I just want to watch the stars for a few minutes." She glanced up at him as he hovered nearby. "Join me, please." She patted the seat cushion on the recliner next to hers.

"Do you know names of any constellations up there?" She pointed at the night sky when he sat down.

"All of the major ones." He nodded. "We use them for navigation when nothing else is available. It's part of the training. The *Leaping Staidus* is the largest one. See those three bright stars over there?" He pointed at them, and she leaned her head closer, peering in that direction at the dark winter sky behind the glass.

Her hair tickled his ear. The sweet flowery smell of her perfume caressed his nostrils, the hint of the warm scent of her skin shot straight to his groin. He shifted his legs, suppressing a groan.

"Yes!" she exclaimed excitedly. "I see them."

"Now, if you follow that line of smaller stars to the left, there is a shorter line underneath that makes the two look kind of like the front paws of a large animal, raised up in the air."

"Wow, an animal, really?" she giggled softly. "All I see are just two rows of stars."

"Me too," he confessed with a laugh. "Whoever came up with those names must've had a crazy imagination."

"And probably had a few drinks on top of that!" she laughed too, leaning away from him, sadly.

He had tamed his erection, but now it was his heart that ached. If he couldn't stand her moving just a couple of hand-lengths away from him, how could he possibly survive the distance between two planets that threatened to separate them next year?

"How do you use the constellations for navigation?" Daisy asked.

He shook off the gloomy thoughts for now.

"The orientation of those three stars is east to west," he explained. "The brightest one on that end always points east. When the sky is clear as it is tonight, it's easy to orientate yourself. On Neron, at least. Other planets' constellations are completely different, of course."

"Have you been to other planets?"

"I've been to two. Aldrai and Tragul."

"Both during the war?"

"To Aldrai as a part of a peaceful delegation. To Tragul both during combat missions and for meetings with Ravil officials. The country of Ravie on Tragul is our ally in the war with *fescods*."

"Isn't the war over now?"

"The *fescods*' invasion of Neron is over, but they refuse to co-exist peacefully with other nations on Tragul. They invaded Ravie and have fought Ravils' resistance for two decades. Taking into account the *fescods*' aggressive nature, they will be causing trouble for a long time still."

"Even losing to Voranians didn't stop them?"

"Nothing truly will, I'm afraid. It's impossible for us to communicate with *fescods*. They don't have a spoken language but communicate with each other through shared brain waves. They're being led by an entity called Central Mind that does all their thinking for them. It uses the individual *fescods* as soldiers—a well-coordinated, ruthless army. It's extremely hard to kill a *fescod*, too. Their skin reflects all energy rays, including laser. Their bodies expel bullets fired from projectile weapons. So far, the most efficient weapons against them have been blades."

"Sounds terrifying." A shudder ran through Daisy's body. "The creatures you ripped to pieces in that video were *fescods*, weren't they?" Her lip curled in disgust. He didn't blame her, *fescods* were rather ugly. Their behaviour made them even more repulsive.

"Yes. The video was taken on Tragul."

"Did you crash there? Your aircraft looked like it'd been in an accident."

"It was shot down. I managed to land it just well enough to survive."

"Oh, no..." she pressed her hands to her chest, her gray-blue eyes rounded in shock. "I had no idea."

"It turned out the unit of *fescods* that attacked me was guarding the main *yirzi* transportation facility. *Yirzi* are a nomad race on Tragul. They have no country to defend and side with whoever pays them more. They had been supplying *fescods* with transportation for their invasion of Neron. My discovery helped cut off resources from the *fescods* on Neron. Which ultimately led to their defeat on our planet."

"That was also how you earned your promotion?"

"Right." In addition to the years of impeccable service, that operation had put him ahead of the line in becoming the Colonel of the Voranian Army.

She sat quietly for a few moments, worrying her plump lower lip with her teeth. He remained silent, too, simply admiring her profile, highlighted by the moonlight.

"You're really proud of that video," she said, understanding flooded her lovely face when she turned it to him.

"It was the highlight of my military career," he agreed. "Or at least the battlefield portion of it."

"That's why you sent it to me. You wanted to share something so important to you with me."

"Well, I've also been told I look good in it. I suppose I wanted to make a good impression on you," he admitted with a smile.

"Oh." She rubbed her forehead. "Of course. You do look…um, fierce in that video."

"I wanted you to like me." He still wanted that. More than ever.

"But I do like you, Colonel."

Normally, he felt a pang of pride when people addressed him by his rank. Not when Daisy did it, though. Hearing his rank from her lips made him feel the distance she'd been maintaining between them more acutely.

She dropped her gaze into her lap, her cheeks took the familiar shade of pink. It happened when she felt angry, he'd learned, or uneasy. Why would Daisy still feel uneasy around him?

"I'm really happy we've managed to become friends after all," she said.

Friends…

That was not what he was hoping for.

"We are friends, Colonel, aren't we?" She gazed at him with a new intensity in her clear eyes.

"Yes," he nearly groaned. "We're friends."

That was a dangerous path to take. He definitely didn't want her as just a friend. But what if she only felt comfortable as a friend in his company?

"I'd better go now." She rose to her feet quickly. "Good night."

And now she was running away from him. Again.

He got up, too, listening to the sound of her light feet taking her up the stairs. Everything inside him urged him to go after her. To grab her, to press her body to his, to claim her. But he'd already tried to do that the night she'd first got here, and she'd almost left him immediately.

He couldn't risk it again. Not now, when losing Daisy would be like ripping his heart out. There had to be a better way.

"Omni," he called to his AI that always was around somewhere. "Get me my tablet, will you?"

He'd earned the admiration of his entire country. However, winning the love and affection of this one woman was proving to be the most difficult operation of his life.

Maybe he had been approaching it all wrong. What if he looked at it as a military battle, with a well-developed plan and strategy? In order to conquer Daisy as his wife, he needed to learn exactly what he was working with and what he was fighting against. He had to learn more about where she came from.

When one of Omni's drones handed him his tablet, he searched for information on humans and their planet Earth. He opened a few pictures and articles on Christmas, the holiday that Daisy spoke about with so much delight and longing tonight.

Maybe he could make the celebration happen for her in Voran? Even if it didn't win him her heart, seeing her eyes sparkle with joy once again would be a reward on its own.

He flipped through the photos and illustration of Christmas celebrations by different Earth nations. There were so many traditions. Tree decorating seemed to be a common theme, though. As were family gatherings and presents.

Most nations claimed to have a magical elderly gentleman visit their houses. Known by many names, he was considered to be kind and brought presents for obedient children.

The disobedient ones were said to be visited by Krampus, in some cultures. Aside from its elongated face, that creature looked remarkably like…a Voranian male.

Horns. Hooves. Thick fur. In some illustrations, Krampus even had the Voranian tongue sticking out—dark-red and long. And the red eyes were…just like his own.

According to the stories, Krampus was not a nice character. He stole and tortured children. And he was called ugly and terrifying.

Grevar's breathing turned rushed and shallow as a dreadful feeling slithered under the fur on his back. Daisy grew up with his exact image being used to scare children. To her, he must look like the reincarnated monster. In fact, he remembered her calling him Krampus once.

Chills spread through his chest. Daisy's shrinking away from his touch suddenly made so much more sense.

He quickly loaded pictures of prominent human males, then filtered them by age and occupation. Similar to Neron, he assumed that popular actors and models would be the embodiment of male beauty on Earth.

Scrolling through the pictures of human males, he became more and more aware of the huge differences between them and him. There were no horns there, no tails or hooves either. No fur. Generally, having any kind of body hair appeared to be unacceptable on Earth, as even the men's chests were completely hairless and smooth in many pictures.

All of them, of course, would have toes and wouldn't mind Daisy having them, either.

Not that he minded human toes himself, contrary to her teasing.

Daisy knew that. She'd become comfortable enough around him to walk in strappy sandals or even barefoot in the house. He had plenty of opportunities to see her toes, and he no longer viewed them as even remotely creepy. He found her toes cute, and he liked how she painted them in different shades of pink or red to match her finger nails.

His biggest worry now was how she viewed *him*. He'd always been confident about his looks. He knew Voranian women found him handsome. For Daisy, however, he must've been a hideous monster all along.

Deep inside, he'd hoped she would become his wife in every sense of the word before the year was up. Now, he feared Daisy would never let him touch her, at all.

What were his options, then? Either she would leave his world for good next year. Or he could try to talk her into staying as the friend she said she was, with no hope of them to ever become more than friends.

Both options would equally break his heart.

Chapter 17

"GOT YOU!" I GRABBED one running little boy and spun him around.

Olvar kicked his hooves in the air squirming and giggling in my arms. His brother got captured by his father just a moment later.

"We won!" the Colonel howled triumphantly, tossing Zun up into the air. The boy laughed and screamed in delight.

"Again! Again! Chase us again!" The kids hopped around us as soon as we'd set them down on the grass of the indoor park where we'd come to have a family picnic.

This was their second weekend at home, and it'd been busy, exhausting, and simply wonderful.

"Lunch now." I shook my head. "We have the Zoo in the afternoon, remember?"

The Ministry's requirements were rather strict. I had to design and maintain a daily schedule, using the guidelines I'd learned during the parenting course. Any serious deviation from the rules could result in the Ministry's revoking the Colonel's right to take the boys home for the weekends, so I made sure to follow them diligently.

The schedule allowed for some flexibility, and that was the time I used for some unplanned fun with the boys. Every kid needed an opportunity to jump around and scream with no rules or regulations, once in a while. So, that was what we did in the park today. Though, wildly running around could still be checked off as physical activity on the schedule for the Ministry.

"I want a cupcake!" Olvar leaped toward the blanket I'd laid out on the grass next to our picnic basket.

"I have three mini cupcakes for each of you. All you have to do is finish Omni's food first."

I removed the lids from the trays with food, handing one to each of the boys, then gave one to the Colonel too. The boys immediately started to shove the food in their mouths without arguing.

Every point on their daily schedule ultimately benefited the children, which made it easier for me to get behind the Voranian system. In a way, it made my life simpler, too, as the twins' nutrition, education, physical activities, and rest time had been regulated. Following the same schedule from birth, the boys had also gotten used to going to bed at a certain time and taking their meals in set intervals.

Running around must've made them work up an appetite. They finished their food in minutes.

"Do you want some more?" I took out the extra tray I'd packed for them, just in case.

"No." They shook their heads. "Cupcakes!"

Grabbing a mini cupcake in each of their little hands, they hopped off, unable to sit still for too long.

"Oh, the energy these two have!" I laughed, watching them skip and roll in the grass.

"I bet anything that they'll fall asleep in the aircraft on the way home." The Colonel stretched out his long legs next to me, balancing his food tray on his muscular thighs.

"They're so stinkin' cute, those two." I got my own food out, too. "It's a good thing I have the Ministry to keep me in check. I would spoil them rotten, otherwise."

"I'm sure they'd take advantage of you, one way or another," he chuckled. "When they look at you with pleading eyes, it's so hard to say no."

In my opinion, the Colonel was fairly strict with his sons. However, the unconditional love between the father and his sons was evident.

I tipped my chin at the food in his lap.

"You better eat it all up. I'm sure they'll make us run a few more miles before the day is over." I stretched my legs in front of me and groaned. "Not sure if my feet can take much more, though. I should've worn my running shoes. These don't have a good arch support."

The Colonel set his empty tray aside, and I handed him a bottle of water.

"Is it hard to walk on feet?" he asked, taking a drink.

I shrugged.

"Not harder than walking on hooves, I imagine."

"Hooves don't get sore from running."

"Lucky for you." I finished my food and put away the container.

"May I?" He suddenly reached for my foot.

I managed only a brief noise of surprise as he grabbed my leg around the ankle then placed my foot into his lap.

"What are you doing?"

"Massage helps relieve muscle ache." He took off my ballet flat, then squeezed my foot in his large hand. "Does it work the same for feet, too?"

"Ohh," I leaned back, propping myself with my hands, as he expertly rubbed my sole and heel. "It most certainly does."

Who would refuse a free foot massage? I forgot all about being self-conscious about my toes in front of a Voranian.

"These are very curious appendages." He gently pulled on each toe, massaging them all in turn. "So cute and tiny."

I lifted an eyebrow in amusement.

"Now, you find them cute? Not repulsive?"

"No part of you could ever repulse me," he said confidently, making my heart skip.

This man. How was I supposed to play cool around him for the rest of our year together, when he made my heart so warm and my body so impossibly hot?

What would I do when the year was up?

Drawing in a long breath, I shoved the worrisome thoughts aside. This had been an amazing morning, and it promised to be an even better day. Humor had helped me get through many awkward moments in life in general and with the Colonel in particular.

"You like my toes?" I teased, wiggling my eyebrows. "Here, I have another set for you." I placed my second foot in his lap, happy to see him laugh as he took my other shoe off.

"Ten times the fun!"

FOR THE AFTERNOON, the Colonel had planned a trip to the Zoo.

The twins jumped with excitement in anticipation, and I kind of did too. I hadn't been to the Voranian Zoo yet. Other than a few small birds and the pretty flying insects in the flower garlands at the mall, I'd seen no local animals.

The Zoo was a group of large glass hemispheres interconnected by arched passageways.

A guide drone accompanied us on our tour. It flew next to us, telling us, in a monotonous, androgynous voice, facts about the Zoo and each of the animals it housed.

After about two hours of browsing the spacious enclosures, I'd seen so many otherworldly animals, it felt like my brain was about to explode from being overloaded with new images and information.

"*Bilgro Uchoit*," the drone hummed, hovering in front of the fenced enclosure with an animal that strongly reminded me of an overinflated tire tube, set on its edge upright. "From the Gaxeon Forest of Neron."

Two eyeballs, suspended on two skinny antennae, extended from the very center of the "tire." As it rolled on its way, hundreds of small black feet where the traction on the tire would be propelled it along.

"*The eyeballs of Bilgro Uchoit are suspended in liquid inside its sealed eyelids. When the animal is moving, its body rotates. However, the eyeballs remain stationary, floating in the clear eyelid capsule.*"

"This one is probably the most bizarre one of all." I gaped at the black, puffy "tires" rolling up and down grassy hills inside their enclosure.

"You said that about the last one, too," Olvar reminded.

Zun found it exceptionally funny for some reason, tossing his head back and laughing exaggeratedly loud.

"The last one was super weird, too," I agreed, remembering the fuzzy orange spiral on six legs. It had expanded, like a released spring, to eat leaves off the tree branches with its mouth located at the higher end of the spring. "Now, I'm confused which one is the most bizarre, to be honest."

"Well, it says here," the Colonel pointed at a holographic display in front of the enclosure, "that *Bilgro Uchoit* obtain nourishment by absorbing nutrients from the dirt with their feet as they move around. So, would that make them half-plant, half-animal?"

"Not sure," I giggled. "But it definitely just made them the most bizarre beings in *my* book."

For a snack, we bought some fruit that looked like a long juicy string curled into a multi-colored spiral.

"Ready to go home?" the Colonel asked as we circled the last glass dome.

The boys were acting much more subdued now, obviously getting tired after the long day of fun.

"The new, limited time exhibition is just ahead," the guide drone informed us. "If you take the north exit to the parking area, you can see it on your way out."

"Can we, please?" Olvar perked up.

"I'm tired," Zun complained.

"What do you think?" The Colonel turned to me.

I shrugged. "Well, since it's on the way, why not? We need to get to the parking garage, anyway."

The Colonel lifted Zun onto his shoulders, and the boy grabbed on to his dad's horns with both hands, like onto the handle bars of a bike.

"Let's go then."

The drone led us through yet another walkway under an arched glass roof. A large crowd gathered inside the next glass dome.

"What's there?" Olvar hopped around me, trying to see between the people.

"Something big," Zun replied. Sitting on his dad's shoulders, he had the best vantage point. "It's moving."

With the hard expression of authority forever etched on his face, the Colonel moved through the crowd with ease, making it part for us. I followed in his wake, firmly holding Olvar by his hand. The boy didn't particularly like being led this way, "like a baby" in his own words. With this many people, however, it would be impossibly hard to locate a five-year-old child if he wondered off.

The "something big" turned out to be the "space blob," like one to those I saw attacking the Colonel in the video he had sent to me.

A *fescod*.

This one seemed even bigger in person than in the video. Its shapeless bulk hulked over the crowd. Skinny protrusions with eyeballs and pincers randomly appeared and disappeared from his body.

Fear ran down my arms in goosebumps when I thought about the Colonel having to face several of them, all on his own.

The creature was on a low platform, surrounded by a glowing metal barrier set with sharp spikes. He appeared agitated, lunging at the barrier with force. Every time the glow touched his concrete-gray skin, it sparked, leaving black scorch marks on his body. The spikes left pale welts on his sides.

He didn't yell, roar or howl, though I was certain the barrier was causing him pain. The complete silence from the *fescod* was eerie and unsettling, especially in contrast with the lively noise of the crowd. The Voranians idly walked by, pausing to take a look at one of the beings who'd invaded their planet and lost.

All battles of that war had been fought far away from the City of Voran, I'd learned. For most people under the dome right now, the *fescod* was not much more than a curious creature, very much like the rest of the exhibits in the Zoo.

"What's that?" Olvar asked, attempting to step closer to the barrier. I held onto his hand tighter, drawing him back to me.

"It's a *fescod*, the species your father fought in the war. Right?" I glanced back at the Colonel for confirmation.

He stared at the *fescod*, his expression dark. I worried that seeing his enemy in person again might trigger something inside the war hero.

"Shall we go?" I asked quietly, touching his arm.

"Yes." He turned away, heading toward the exit.

"They shouldn't have him here," he said as we walked down one of the narrow walkways toward the parking garage.

"Because he is a sentient being displayed like an animal in the Zoo?" I asked.

"No," he bit off. "Because it's not safe for the public."

"Oh."

"*Fescods'* intelligence is in their Common Mind. Once cut off from its signal, they aren't capable of processing problems or creating solutions. The debate about whether they're even self-aware is still ongoing. That must be what allowed the Zoo to organize this exhibition in the first place."

"So, without their 'mind,' they aren't intelligent enough to attack?" I asked, hurrying next to him down the walkway.

"Oh, they attack any chance they get. An individual *fescod* is not much more than a mindless robot, unable to plan or organize without the Mind. His inherent aggression, however, still makes him very dangerous. The barrier they have is not adequate to contain an enraged *fes-*

cod. He's aggravated by it. It's only a matter of time before he gets angry enough to break through it. I'll need to talk to Drustan about this. As the Governor, he would be able to put a stop to this."

A sudden noise came from behind us. Screams of panic and the thundering sound of hooves rushed in our direction.

"What's going on?" I turned around to look back.

"Come." The Colonel promptly grabbed me by my arm, dragging me toward the end of the walkway, which still was quite far away. "Faster." He broke into a jog, forcing me to keep up, Olvar running beside me.

The crowd around us thickened, nearly blocking the narrow passage.

"*Fescod*! *Fescod* broke loose!" Voranians screamed, rushing to the exit along the walkway and sweeping us with them.

"Oh no!" Just what the Colonel had been worried about. And it had happened even faster than he'd predicted.

"Keep moving, Daisy!" the Colonel shouted.

I concentrated on not losing the sight of his carved horns as the crowd spilled between us, separating me from him. In the chaos, I didn't even realize when Olvar's hand had slipped out of mine.

"Olvar!" I screamed in horror, noticing that he was gone. Peering through the mass of panicking people, I searched for the little boy. "Come back! Where are you?"

"Daisy." The Colonel made his way to me. Wrapping an arm around me, he half-carried me to the exit then finally out of the tunnel and onto the parking platform. He then pushed me to the wall around the corner, away from the Voranians rushing by.

"Olvar!" I fought his grip, desperate to run back inside the glass tunnel. "He's back there. Olvar!"

Pure horror flashed through the Colonel's expression, then his calm focus returned.

"Here." He took Zun off his shoulders, handing him to me. "Take Zun to the aircraft. You two get inside and lock the doors. Stay there, until I come back. Don't get out, no matter what happens. Understood?"

I nodded rapidly several times, clutching Zun to me. "Oh God, please find him."

"I will." He rushed off, heading back into the tunnel against the rushing crowd.

"Come, baby," I muttered to Zun.

Holding him to my chest, I ran, keeping close to the wall for as long as was possible. I refused to set Zun down, even as he seemed to grow heavier in my arms by the minute. Dodging the people who dashed all around us, I turned toward the centre of the parking platform where our aircraft was located.

"Here we go." I clicked the doors open as soon as I reached the aircraft. "You come right here, honey." I put Zun into his seat and buckled him in.

"Where is daddy?" the boy's voice was so tiny, it made my eyes swell with tears as the inside of my nose prickled.

"He'll be right back, sweetheart. He'll just need to—"

Something enormous slammed at me from the side. The air was knocked out of my chest. Every single bone in my body seemed to crack and shutter as I crashed to the ground.

"Zun! Lock the doors, baby!" I screamed.

A huge, shapeless, gray mass moved over me, blocking my view of the boy...and the world around me.

※

GREVAR

"Olvar!"

Shoving people out of his way, he moved against the current of the panicking crowd. A few of the Zoo security personnel joined him, trying to make their way back to the *fescod* exhibit.

They should've been there all along. Bitterness fueled his anger at the failure of the management to foresee this. If they had only consulted someone who'd actually been to war with those things. If anyone had only asked *him* before deciding it was a good idea to exhibit a *fescod*, seething with aggression, for the peaceful weekend crowd.

"Olvar! Where are you?"

"Daddy!" a child's voice came from up ahead.

Olvar!

He increased his efforts, moving faster while pushing against the avalanche of people. Squeezing all the way to the wall, he saw his son up ahead. Curled against a support arch, Olvar crouched low to the floor by the wall. It was a miracle he'd managed to escape a crushing blow from one of the many hooves rushing by.

Grevar couldn't get to him yet, though. The crowd seemed to be thickening by the minute.

"Is he yours?" a man in bright civilian clothing asked, scooping Olvar off the floor.

"Yes!"

"Daddy!" The boy reached for him over the moving forest of horns.

"Come here, you." He snatched his son from the stranger.

"Hurry," the man said urgently. "Get him out of here. The monster back there has been trampling over anyone who tried to stop him."

Fescods weren't easy to stop. With no necks to snap or heads to smash, with thick skin, and all their appendages often completely hidden inside their bodies, they were nearly invincible. Someone who had never faced them in a battle before wouldn't know what to do.

Well, at least the Zoo security had the right weapons on them as they rushed past. They should be able to stop the carnage.

His priority was to get his family to safety as soon as possible.

Carrying his son under his arm, Grevar hurried back to the parking platform.

Out of the tunnel again, he headed straight in the direction of their aircraft. First, he had to get his family out of danger, then he'd have to see what could be done about the raging *fescod* on the loose.

He stopped in his tracks at the sight of the amorphous body of the *fescod* suddenly rolling out of another walkway and onto the parking platform.

Then, his heart nearly skidded to a stop as the creature rammed into Daisy at full speed, knocking her off her feet. Before the *fescod* had a chance to go after Zun, who was gaping at him in horror strapped to his seat inside the aircraft, Daisy screamed, diverting the creature's attention back to herself. Zun slammed on the button, lowering the door.

Sprouting long protrusions tipped with sharp pincers, the *fescod* rolled over to Daisy.

His wife screamed again, making his blood curdle with horror.

Putting Olvar down, Grevar remotely clicked open the aircraft door on the opposite side of the *fescod*.

"To the aircraft." He gently pushed his son in that direction. "Lock the doors behind you."

The boy nodded, a somber focus on his little face. The Academy's training must've kicked in, as his son sprinted to the aircraft at full speed, then jumped inside it and hit the door lock button—all without a word of fear or protest.

At the same moment, Grevar charged the *fescod*.

The old, familiar rage flared high. Only this time, it seemed a million times stronger as it was fanned by fear. Fear for his wife. The horror of any harm done to her blinded him as he rammed his horns into the *fescod's* meaty side at full speed.

Shoved to his side and away from Daisy, the alien switched his attention and his pincers to Grevar.

Dark blood gushed from the two puncture wounds left by Grevar's horns.

Since his claws had been filed to better suit the peaceful life in Voran, Grevar was unable to pierce through the *fescod's* thick skin by using his hands. His fingers slipped, getting no grip on the bulging mass.

The *fescod's* pincers dug into Grevar's arms and shoulders, tearing at his clothes and his flesh underneath.

He growled in agony, shoving against his enemy with all his might. They rolled on the ground together. Clawing at the *fescod's* skin, his hands slick with the creature's blood, he stuck one finger into the wound left by his horns then quickly inserted another finger.

The massive bulk of the *fescod* shuddered with pain as Grevar sank his fingers deeper. The pincers ferociously ripped at his army coat, fur, and flesh, but Grevar wouldn't let go.

Yanking at the edges of the wound, he ripped the *fescod's* flesh open. It quivered under his fingers when he reached inside with both hands. Feeling the cluster of *fescod's* beating hearts inside, he wrapped his fingers around it and ripped them all out in one hard yank.

The *fascod's* convulsing body slumped, spreading into a shapeless heap of torn flesh on the ground. He collapsed on top of it, catching his breath, his hands shaking from strain and stress.

"Grevar..." Daisy crawled over to him, climbing up the grisly mess that used to be the *fescod*. "Please, please tell me you're okay."

She touched his face. Fear and worry floated in her *lilcae*-colored eyes.

Did she even realize she'd just called him by his first name? For the first time ever?

He wrapped his arm around her shoulders drawing her into his side.

His boys were safe, and his wife was in his arms.

"I'm fine, sweetheart." He smiled at her. "Better than ever."

Chapter 18

GREVAR'S INJURIES WERE treated right there at the Zoo. My own toll after the ordeal with the *fescod*, miraculously, turned out to be just shock and a few bruises. Thankfully, both children were completely unharmed. After the two of us gave our statements to the Security Forces, we were free to go home.

From the aircraft, Grevar called the Governor Drustan, telling him in no uncertain terms exactly what he thought about displaying their war enemies in public places.

I fed the children dinner from the food container given to us by the Zoo officials. Extremely excited after having watched their dad "punch the bad guy," the boys had taken a while to settle down in the aircraft. Utterly exhausted, however, they had only made it to the main room after we came home, passing out on the couch on top of each other.

His arm draped over my shoulders, I helped Grevar upstairs to his bedroom, then led him into his bathroom.

Letting go of me, he sat on the edge of the tub while I ordered Omni to fill it.

"I must look like the true Krampus to you," he chuckled. "Hideous and covered in gore."

"No." I shook my head, helping him take off his blood-soaked army coat. "When I look at you, I don't see the Krampus, Grevar. I see a man who selflessly defended his family. Who saved me. And I admire that man, deeply."

Peeling his blood-stained shirt off, I hovered my fingers over the wounds on his shoulders. They all had been treated. The cuts and gashes in his skin had been covered by a protective healing film. The fur around the wounds, however, remained crusted with dried blood.

"Daisy," he exhaled, suddenly circling my waist with his arms and pressing his face to my stomach.

Standing silently, I raked my fingers through the trimmed fur on the back of his head, trying to imagine what he must be going through. He'd spent years fighting the enemy who'd invaded his home world, only to have to fight it once again in the heart of his city, during the peaceful times.

His hand unexpectedly slid from my waist down to my backside, cupping my ass cheek. With a low groan, he pressed me closer.

"Grevar," I said quietly, soothingly stroking the fur over his shoulder blades. "The bath is full, now. You need to rest tonight."

It was hard *not* to follow his lead, now that he finally held me with passion. He'd been in my thoughts constantly. Even without the fancy technology of the Dream Spa, I saw him in my dreams every single night. I wanted him, badly.

No way was I taking advantage of him in this state, though. I wished for this to be more than a quick fuck after a stressful day. If we had sex, I wanted his mind and his heart to be into it too, not just his body.

I cared too much about this man to become the mistake he might regret in the morning.

"I'll have to take the kids to bed," I said, gently leaning away. Tearing my hands from him, I stepped toward the exit.

He didn't hold me back and didn't stop me. Before leaving, I glanced over my shoulder at him.

Bloodied and bruised, and gloriously undefeated, he sat on the edge of the tub, following my every move with those wonderful red eyes.

"Thank you, Grevar," I said softly but clearly. "Thank you for saving my life and for everything you've done for me." I was not going to let this slip by, though. "Sleep well. We'll talk about everything in the morning."

Grevar had become so close to me, I felt I could talk to him about anything. Whatever it was that had been keeping him away from me, we could talk about that too. We'd deal with it, just as we'd dealt with other things. I had faith that together, we could work it all out.

Walking back downstairs to put our children to bed, I realized that Shula was right. This was my home, my family, and my husband. Grevar and I had created a home in his house. We were raising *our* children. And we shared a loving, caring relationship with each other, whether or not we'd had sex...*yet*.

I had everything I'd ever dreamed of and more. My journey to Voran hadn't been a failure, after all, but the biggest success of my life.

<u>GREVAR</u>

"Get me the tablet, Omni," he ordered to the AI.

He'd washed all the blood and gore off his body, but remained in the tub, letting the warm water sooth his aching muscles.

There was no way Daisy was leaving Voran next year, he'd decided.

She liked it here, he was positive about that. She loved his children to the point of being ready to die for them, she'd proven that today. They absolutely adored her, too. She'd confessed he had her friendship, gratitude, and admiration. But he wanted all of her. Her heart and her body, too. He would do everything it took to make her see him as someone more than just a friend, as her husband and her lover too.

Christmas, the holiday she had been talking about was tomorrow, and he had a surprise for her. Because that was how humans made gifts to each other—they kept them a secret until the moment they gave them to each other.

He wasn't sure exactly why Earthlings did it that way, but if Daisy would get more excited just because he had kept her presents a secret, then so it was going to be. During the past week, he'd been searching and buying presents for Daisy, and he had to admit, it'd been fun to guess what she might like. Omni had been hiding all the pretty things Grevar had found for her so far.

Turning on the tablet, he checked on the delivery of the giant *maikai* tree he'd ordered. It was supposed to arrive early in the morning.

Lievoa was coming over for breakfast tomorrow, and his dad and brothers would be arriving later in the afternoon.

Daisy would have her very first Christmas on Neron. And he was determined for it not to be her last one in his house. All her Christmases should be celebrated with him and his boys, because they were a family now. Shula gave him the twins, but Daisy made all of them a much happier family. Their world would never be complete without her anymore.

She had to stay.

None of what he'd planned and organized seemed adequate, though. Something else was needed, something bigger. Something that would help him keep her in Voran for sure.

Lievoa had given him an idea.

On his tablet, he requested the information about the Central Mall. This place was bigger, with better security than the Eastern Mall his cousin had suggested. It was also closer to their house and directly on his way to work.

Most stores were closed now, but the mall AI would be available to answer his questions.

He clicked on the contact button for property lease inquiries.

Daisy had wanted to have her own bakery. He would help her get started. With her talent and perseverance, he had no doubt she'd make it a success. She'd stay after the year was up, and he'd have all the time he needed to convince her he was worthy to be her husband in every sense of that word. Then he'd spend the rest of his life making her happy.

He scheduled viewing appointments for three of the available properties at the Central Mall, for the day after tomorrow. After work, he'd take Daisy to see them all and choose which one she liked the best.

Feeling better about the situation now that he had a plan, he was about to turn off the tablet when a message from the mall AI popped up.

"Would you like to see the specials or to book follow-up appointments with the previously visited businesses?"

A list of the stores and services scrolled by. Judging by the date, these were the places that Daisy had visited during her shopping trip with Lievoa.

Except for the Dream Spa. That one must have been there still from when he had visited the establishment a few times earlier. Long before Daisy came into his life, he would go to the spa on the nights when staying at home felt exceptionally lonely and he craved the intimacy beyond what his own hand could deliver. Those lucid dreams had been fun. Except that at the end of the day, he would still return to his empty house. Alone.

Upon a closer look, the day of the last visit puzzled him. It was the same date as Daisy's shopping trip. He pulled up the statement of his credit account. Sure enough, there was a corresponding charge for it on that day.

Blood heated in his veins from the realization that it was his wife who had paid the visit to the spa that day. Why would she do that? When she had him, the breathing, living—and lately, perpetually aroused—husband at home?

"One day, you will want to be fucked by a man. And it could only be me," he'd told her long ago.

The fact that she had gone to that place instead of coming to him burned through his pride and dignity like acid. Did she despise him so much that she preferred a machine to his touch?

After everything they had been through together.

After what she'd just said to him tonight.

Whether or not they shared a bed, Daisy was his. She belonged to him, body and soul, she just needed a little more time to realize that, and he was willing to give her the time.

If she were to dream about another man during this time, however, all his efforts would be lost. Then, she'd leave...

He thought about the life they had already built together here in *their* home. How comfortable they had become with each other. He couldn't imagine this house without her.

"She could've simply gotten a massage to relax her muscles," he told himself, trying to fight the poison of jealousy flooding his veins.

Then he thought about the change in her behaviour of late. How oddly skittish she had become. Talkative by nature, she would suddenly fall silent. Whenever they touched, even accidentally, she would pull away quickly.

If there was another man...

He groaned, sitting up in the tub. The water splashed over, just like his anger bubbling over inside him. What hurt the most was that she had done this behind his back. While all his thoughts had been about her, she'd been dreaming about someone else.

"I need to see the footage of the last visit charged to my credit account," he typed the message to the Dream Spa AI.

Knowing it would only hurt more, he couldn't stop. He needed to know everything, now. The whole entire fucking truth, no matter if it was about to destroy him.

"Due to our privacy policy, we need to confirm your ID, please," a reply came.

"It's my fucking account!" he growled, climbing out of the tub and leaving puddles of water everywhere. "And my own wife!"

Stomping into the bedroom, he got the credit bracelet and his ID, then scanned them both for the AI.

"One moment, please."

Clutching the tablet in his hand, he paced the floor, dripping water on the rug. He waited for the video to load, expecting his heart to break into a million little pieces any moment, now.

Hitting *play*, he braced himself for the image of one of those human men from Earth with their clean-shaven chests. They'd be holding *his* wife in their furless arms.

His own scowling face appeared on the screen instead, making him think he was somehow staring at his reflection, at first.

The image zoomed out, then, showing his shirtless torso.

"Oh no…" Daisy's voice reached him, confirming he was now watching her no-longer secret fantasy.

Tablet clamped in his numb fingers, he plopped on the bed in shock.

Daisy, his sweet little flower, had been fantasizing about being pounded hard by someone who looked an awful lot like him.

It *was* him, his "fierce" red eyes included.

He watched for another moment, giving his brain the time to catch up with what he was seeing. However, his cock caught on with what was happening first, jumping to attention, hard like steel.

Should he even be watching this? Let alone getting hard to the video of the naked Daisy now being hammered from behind. Somewhere deep inside, a small voice whispered belatedly that he shouldn't be intruding on her private fantasies.

"This is my fucking face, right there!" he snapped at his inner voice, pointing at the image on the screen. "I *am* already involved. More that I fucking knew!"

He should've known. How had he been so blind? So clueless? For so long? He'd read all her signs wrong.

"It's my fantasy, too."

And it was time to make fantasy a reality.

He stopped the video.

"Is there anything else we can do for you?" the AI prompted.

"No," he gritted through his teeth, "but *I* can."

Chapter 19

<u>GREVAR</u>

He found her in front of the mirror in his old bedroom, brushing her amazing orange hair. She was wearing a much more modest nightshirt this time, something that actually concealed most of her body from view.

But not for long.

He lunged for her straight from the doorway, dying to hold her. No doubts marred his mind any longer.

Her big eyes grew even bigger at the sight of him butt-naked, bath water dripping from his fur.

"Please, don't say no." He gathered her in his arms at last.

Her chest rose with a deep breath. Lifting her arms, she wrapped them around his neck.

"Yes," she exhaled. "Grevar. Honey. A million times *yes*."

Finally.

It felt like a huge boulder that had been pressing down on all his hopes and plans for the future had rolled away, letting him breathe freely once again.

He buried his face in her neck, breathing in her scent, her warmth, and her sweetness.

"Grevar?" She stroked his back. "How are you feeling, darling? Are you sure that's what you want? Right now?"

"I've been sure about what *I* want for a long time." He slipped his hands under her nightshirt, squeezing her round backside. "Now, that I know exactly what *you* want, nothing is going to hold me back."

"What *do* I want?" She leaned back, catching his eyes, a teasing spark flashing in hers.

"Me," he growled, lifting her up onto the dresser. Her legs fell open, making room for him to get closer. "You want *me*."

The full meaning of his own words rolled through his chest with surprise and pleasure. He still couldn't believe his Daisy was not repulsed but aroused at the sight of him.

She moaned, as if to confirm it again, and he slid his hand up her thigh. Dipping his thumb between her legs, he found her warm and slick already. His heart swelled with pride and delight as another shot of lust surged to his groin.

"Tell me," he rasped, hiking her shirt up to her waist. "Have you been thinking about me, right now?"

"Always," she murmured, her cheeks turning that delicate shade of pink they often did when she was angry, or embarrassed, or...aroused as it turned out. "I *cannot* stop thinking about you. I've tried but...All those naughty thoughts..."

"Good." He slid his hand up her body, palming her breast—full and warm in his grip.

"Oh, I want you, Grevar," she moaned, when he softly plucked her nipple. Wrapping her legs around his middle, she pressed herself to him, rubbing her core against his erection.

Lust blinded him. His mind swam with need for her.

"This one will be quick," he warned, fitting himself between her thighs. "You drive me wild. I feel like I'll explode any minute." Everything in him was on fire, ready to explode—his mind, his heart, his cock. "But I want to come inside you."

Cupping her backside, he slid her forward along the top of the dresser, impaling her on his cock.

"You *are* huge!" she gasped, biting her bottom lip.

"Is it just like you've imagined?" he asked, giving her a moment to adjust before thrusting just a little deeper.

"Oh no, better." She breathed heavily. "So much better. Please, don't stop."

He couldn't stop, even if he'd tried.

Buried balls deep in her slick warmth felt incredible, the orgasm was teasing him already. Pumping his hips, he let his desire for her overtake him. It spread like warm sunshine through his entire body, growing hotter with each passionate thrust.

"Yes," she whimpered, fisting her fingers in the thick fur on his shoulders. "Oh God, yes..."

Gripping her ass, he pumped harder.

Her body tensed. Her legs flexed, holding him in a vise as she arched her back. Sliding his hand up, he found her breast under her nightshirt. Cupping it, he slightly pinched her pebbling nipple, tipping her over the edge.

Breathing in sharp gasps, she came around him. Her muscles clenched, bringing on the explosion of his own climax. The pleasure rippled through him, rocking his body and blowing his mind.

Clutching her to his chest with one arm, he roared and slammed his hand into the mirror behind her.

The dresser shook. The mirror shattered, raining shards to the floor.

"Oh no! Not again." Daisy glanced back over her shoulder. "Do you always end sex with breaking things?"

"End? Sweetheart, this is just the beginning."

I CLUNG TO HIS SHOULDERS as he carried me to bed.

"Now, I can take my time." He laid me down on the bed. "I want to see all of you." He grabbed the hem of my white cotton nightshirt and took it off over my head.

He then sat back on his haunches, sliding his glowing gaze down my body.

"So?" I exhaled a nervous giggle, since he just stared at me, not saying a word. "What do you think?"

"You're breathtakingly beautiful." Splaying his hand on my stomach, he slid it up to the valley between my breasts. "Your skin is glowing in the moonlight."

I didn't know my Colonel could be this poetic. I wasn't sure about the glowing part, but my skin tingled with warmth and my chest heated with pleasure from his attention and the admiration in his eyes.

"Do you find me odd? Different from what you're used to?" I asked.

"*Special*, my Daisy-flower, not odd." He shook his head. "You are nothing like anyone I've ever seen. You make me feel like no one else, too. You are *you*—beautiful, kind, and unique. And I wouldn't have you any other way."

He was unique for me, too. One of a kind. And it had very little to do with his otherworldly looks.

Now that I finally had him, I wanted to explore every inch of his marvelous body. I slid my hands up his abs—carved granite, covered by short velvety fur. It was considerably thicker and longer over his pecs.

A trail of longer fur also ran from his belly button down to his magnificent erection that bobbed hard and strong again. I stared at it for a moment, wondering how it had ever fit inside me in the first place. The sensation of being stretched impossibly wide lingered between my legs, tingling with a renewed rush of need.

He leaned lower, gently trailing his lips along my skin, just below my ear.

"Kiss me, Grevar," I whispered, fisting my hands in the fur on the back of his head.

With a groan, he took my mouth, pressing his chest to mine. His fur tickled my erect nipples. The tip of his tongue slipped past my lips, and I met it with my tongue. Arching my back, I longed to press every inch of my body to his.

His hands seemed to be everywhere at once. Massaging my breasts, squeezing my ass, gliding along my skin with increasing urgency.

His long tongue wrapped around mine, and I moaned into his mouth. He broke the kiss, leaning back to see my face.

"Don't stop," I begged. "I want to feel your tongue...everywhere."

He gave me a lop-sided grin. "I'd love to taste all of you, too."

Shifting down my body, he circled the tip of my breast with the tapered tip of his tongue. With a flash of heat in his flaming eyes he tightened the circle, squeezing my nipple in the noose of his slick, hot tongue.

"Wow..." I undulated under him, riding the wave of pleasure that rolled over me. "This is just...wow."

"You like that?" he asked smugly, before switching to another breast, playing with it by squeezing, pulling, and flicking the nipple with his tongue.

"Oh, God, yes..." I panted. From the moment I'd first seen his tongue, I'd been intrigued by its potential. "I had no idea you could use it like that." His tongue turned out to be a perfect tool for delivering pleasure, and he wielded it with skill and confidence, driving me mad with lust.

"You just wait..." he murmured, sliding further down.

Hands on my knees, he opened my legs then dove between my thighs.

I gasped loudly as his tongue slipped inside me. The tip circled the walls of my opening, teasing the spot inside me that made my knees tremble from intense pleasure.

He leaned closer, rubbing the sensitive spot between my folds with the thicker base of his tongue.

I moaned and writhed from the double-pleasure. He gripped my hips, keeping me steady for the assault of ecstasy.

Waves of bliss rolled through my body, building up. The achy pressure grew unbearable. Gripping his horns, I lifted my hips up, fully giving myself to his mouth and tongue. He moved it faster, rubbing harder, and I exploded with pleasure, coming hard.

Panting, I let the swells of my orgasm roll through me, as he twirled his marvelous tongue in and out of me, reaping every last shudder of pleasure, again and again.

Letting go of his horns, I dropped my arms to the side. Staring up to the starry sky above us through the lace of the flowering garlands of the canopy, I felt as if I were floating, descending from the crest of passion.

"This was just..." I whispered, my veins filling with languid warmth, making me unable to move a muscle. "Out of this world, truly."

I had no desire to move. I could have stayed like that forever, spread on the bed like a starfish, with Grevar's face between my legs.

He chuckled, shifting up my body. The tip of his tongue flicked out, licking my juices off his glistening lips.

I took his face between my hands.

"I'm falling for you, Grevar," I confessed, baring my heart to him. "Hopelessly fast."

His expression turned serious, his eyes flickering between mine.

"Daisy. I'm already there."

Breath hitched in my throat. He gave me no chance to reply, claiming my mouth with his again.

He kissed me with tender passion, as if he were putting into his kiss all the things he couldn't express in words. Holding me in his arms, he let his tail stroke my sides, trailing its pointed tip up and down my hips and ribs.

The desire for him always smouldered just under my skin, and the orgasms he'd given me hadn't done much to extinguish it. With his kisses and caresses, it flamed higher, slowly taking over again.

Clearly, I couldn't get enough of this man, now that I'd finally got him into my bed.

A moan escaped my throat. My legs fell apart again, as if on their own, cradling him. His straining erection pressed between my legs, sending a shiver of anticipation through me.

"You're not done with me yet?" he chuckled, guessing my unquenchable desire for him.

"I don't think I'll ever be done with you," I murmured. "I've wanted you for so long."

"I wish for nothing else but to spend the rest of my life buried inside you." With a last nibble on my bottom lip, he moved lower, trailing his tongue down my neck.

Sucking the tip of one of my breasts into his mouth, he teased the nipple with his teeth.

The post-orgasmic languid glow was gone. Burning hot lust filled me.

"More..." I panted. "I need more..."

He rose over me, lifting an eyebrow.

"I know what you need." A dangerous spark heated his gaze.

Grabbing my hips, he flipped me over.

I made a startled noise of surprise as he yanked my bum up, positioning my hips over his lap. Hands splayed on my backside, he slid them up and down, rubbing my butt cheeks.

"So smooth and soft," he murmured under his breath. His thumbs pressed against my tail bone. "With no tail to conceal a thing."

He lowered his head. His tongue trailed along my skin, down to my slit. Then I felt a bite of his teeth on one of my ass cheeks.

I trembled head to toe with anticipation when the tip of his tail slid between my legs.

"Grevar..." I whimpered, shifting my hips closer to him." Please..."

He growled in response, rising to his knees. The tip of his rock-hard erection pressed against my opening as he positioned himself behind me.

"Is that how you want it?" His voice deep and low, he shoved me against him, sliding inside me in one thrust.

A groan vibrated in my throat. The achy pressure of being stretched so impossibly tight around his massive girth made the need spike through my lower belly. "Yes!"

He grabbed a handful of my hair, tilting my head back. I whimpered from the stinging pain and prickling pleasure. My body lit up with excitement, every nerve in my skin buzzed with thrill.

"My. Little. Daisy-flower. Likes. To be. Pounded," He slammed into me, punctuating each word with a thrust. "Hard and Rough."

Moaning like a woman possessed, I gripped one of the canopy posts, bracing against his furious thrusts. He caught one of my swaying breasts in his large hand, squeezing the tip between his fingers.

I screamed as the charge of intense pleasure shot through me like lightning. The orgasm hit me, suddenly all at once.

My screams drowned in the deafening roar from his chest as he pumped his release into me, not slowing down his speed.

Propped on one arm, he held me tight with the other, curling his body over mine while the orgasm rocked through both of us.

His arm shook, and he rolled to the side, taking me with him. Wrapped in his large body, his arms around me, the soft fur of his chest warming my back, I snuggled into him. His chest rose and fell rapidly, mine did too, as we both caught our breath.

"Was it how you've imagined it would be?" he asked, panting. "Back at the Dream Spa?"

I tensed. "How do you know about that?"

He kissed my hair, gently stroking my arm. "I requested to watch the video."

Blood rushed to my face, though we'd gone way past the point for me to be mortified. What he'd just done to me was a million times more intense and intimate than my dream at the spa.

Still, I mumbled, "That was kinda private..."

"It shouldn't have been. You should've come to me, right away. I'm your husband, it's my duty to deliver your pleasure in any way you wish."

"You see right there?" I twisted in his arms to face him. "If from the very beginning you spoke a little less of duty and a little more of your true feelings for me, all of this could be different."

"Well, if you have ever asked me about my feelings, instead of accusing me of forcing myself on you—"

"Oh, now it's all my fault?" I rose on my arm over him as my temper heated.

"Daisy?" he asked in a softer tone. "Would you want for this to be different?"

His question made me pause. Right now, lying in bed next to the naked Grevar, I loved everything about this moment just the way it was.

"No. Of course not."

His stern expression melted into a smile.

"Come here." He pulled me into his chest. "All of this *is* your fault, sweetheart. From the moment you showed up here, my life has been turned upside down." He kissed my face. "And I wouldn't have it any other way."

My anger evaporated before it even had a chance to really form.

"You *are* my dream man, Grevar." I relaxed on his wide chest. "Being with you is much better than any dream. And the best part is that you're here to stay."

Chapter 20

A RAY OF SUNSHINE MADE its way through the garland canopy. It fell on my face, warming my skin and making me smile. It happened every morning when the sky was clear, but something was different today.

I rolled to my back, stretching through the new ache in my body. I was so deliciously sore this morning, after being so blatantly claimed and thoroughly loved by Grevar last night. My smile stretched wider. Blush heated my cheeks as the memories flooded my mind.

I patted the bed in search of him. Not finding him at my side, I opened my eyes.

It was late morning already. I'd slept in. I jumped out of bed then winced at a tug of soreness through my muscles. Today, apparently, I would need to move a little slower than normal. The thought made me smile again.

Grevar and the boys must be up already. Both kids seemed absolutely exhausted after the events at the Zoo yesterday. The full impact of what they'd witnessed remained to be seen. However, it wouldn't be surprising if they had trouble sleeping after that.

Worried about the children and eager to see their father, I put on a dress from the closet, brushed my hair, and slipped on a pair of comfy flat-sole shoes.

"Omni, where is the Colonel?" I asked, taking one last look at my reflection in the mirror.

The AI's screen came to life.

"The Colonel is downstairs, in the main room, Madam Kyradus."

The sound of Grevar's name when used to address me had stopped bothering me a while ago. Now, it made my chest warm with pleasure.

I decided I was keeping his name, if just as another sign that he and I belonged together.

"And the boys?" I headed toward the doors.

"They are downstairs, too. As is Madam Lievoa Kyradus."

"Lievoa is here?"

"Yes."

She must have heard about the incident at the Zoo and came to check on her cousin and nephews. We'll have a family brunch together, then.

With that on my mind, I opened the bedroom door and...gasped.

A humongous tree rose from the main room's floor all the way up to the highest point of the biggest glass dome. I had never seen anything like it before.

Its lime-green needles were as long as my forearm and as thick as my finger. All possible kinds of things dangled from them, from brightly-colored toys, to gilded tea cups, to flower garlands and wrapped presents of all sizes.

Several drones flew around it, placing more pretty items on its sprawling branches.

"Merry Christmas!" Shouts came from downstairs as I descended, admiring the tree.

Grevar stood at the base of the tree in the main room. The twins energetically bounced around him, clapping their hands. Lievoa smiled and waved at me from the couch.

"Isn't it amazing?" She gestured at the tree. "I love it!"

"I do, too." I rushed down the stairs. "This is just..."

"It's going to be like having two Victory Days in a year!" Olvar exclaimed, throwing his arms up in the air.

"One is warm! And one is with a big, pretty tree!" his brother added with delight.

Hands in his pockets, Grevar shifted his weight from hoof to hoof.

"So, you like it?" he asked as I came closer.

"Do I?" I choked up, thinking about the effort he'd gone through to make Christmas happen for me in Voran. My chest flooded with gratitude, and my face flushed from pleasure.

"You're blushing again," he said, tentatively. "It can mean so many things with you."

"I love it!" I jumped into his arms, hugging his neck. "Thank you so much." I kissed his face.

He laughed, spinning me through the room in his arms.

"The best is yet to come." He set me down. "This is going to be a great day. I promise."

I glanced up at the gigantic tree.

"Oh. Wait a moment!" I dashed back up the stairs. Grabbing the small purse off my night table, I ran back down again.

"Here." I took out Grandma's ornament and hung it on the highest tree branch I could reach. I stepped back, admiring the way the red-and-gold ornament from Earth glistened prettily among the lime-green needles of the tree from Neron. "It belongs here."

Grevar hugged me from behind.

"And you belong right here, Daisy." He kissed my temple. "In my arms."

"With us!" The boys jumped around, nudging me with their cute, little horns. "Us, too!"

This was now my home.

Better than I could have ever dreamed of.

EPILOGUE

TWO YEARS LATER

"Time to get up." Grevar's furry, muscular arm circled me.

"Already?" I stretched, rolling to my back, as he nuzzled the side of my face then sat on the bed.

"Mhm. We'll be leaving straight after breakfast." His hand splayed on my rounded belly, he asked as he'd been asking me daily for the past five months now, "How are you feeling?"

I blinked my eyes open, met his gaze, and smiled.

"Well, good, I guess. I haven't thrown up yet, today."

"And how is my baby girl?" His voice softened as he gently patted my stomach.

The baby in my belly didn't have a drop of Voranian blood. She had been conceived by artificial insemination using the human sperm Grevar and I had ordered from Earth, after selecting an anonymous donor together.

Yet from the moment we'd heard her heartbeat from the monitor in the doctor's office, Grevar acted as any expectant father would—maybe even a little bit crazier than most.

He had her in-womb images framed. He sang lullabies to my belly. And he crossed out days on the paper calendar he'd ordered specifically for that purpose, impatiently waiting for her due date.

"She is quiet." I rubbed the side of my belly where she often kicked me when awake. "Probably sleeping still since there is no one to wake *her* up in there." I swung one of my legs his way, playfully nudging him in the shoulder with my foot.

He caught it with his hand.

"We need to hurry up." He said. "You'd be really sorry if you miss my surprise."

Somehow, he'd learned about humans keeping presents a secret until a special day, and he never failed to torture me with anticipation.

"Can't you tell me what it is and put me out of my misery?" I begged.

"It won't be a surprise then if I tell, would it?"

"Please?" I batted my eyelashes at him.

"Nope."

"You are insufferable." I swung my other leg at him, and he caught my foot before it touched his arm.

A flash of heat sparked in his eyes as he held both my feet at his shoulders, facing me.

"Well, if you insist on staying in bed..." He rubbed his chin against the side of my sole.

I giggled at the tickling of his beard and struggled to free my foot from his grip, but he held it firmly.

"We can skip the surprise." He gently bit down on my toe, sending a rush of a very different type of anticipation through me.

"Tempting..." Spending an entire day in bed with my husband always seemed like a good idea. "But it's Christmas Day—"

"Exactly. Up!" He jumped out of bed, scooping me up and setting me down on the floor in one fluid movement. "We have a few hours before we need to pick up the kids."

Christmas didn't fall on a weekend this year. Grevar had arranged with the Academy to get the boys after their morning lessons and bring them back to the school tomorrow afternoon.

"Oh boy, Christmas surprise." I went to the bathroom to get ready. "I can't wait!"

"YOU'RE STILL NOT GOING to tell me where we're going?" I asked, glancing at Grevar as the cityscape of Voran floated under our aircraft.

"No." He shook his head.

"It must be something really fancy." I smoothed the silky material of the gorgeous, ivory-colored dress over my knees. It had been a part of the surprise. Grevar presented it to me this morning, along with a pair of gold, crystal-studded sandals to wear with it.

"You'll see." He was wearing his dress uniform, his horns polished to a shine.

The aircraft started to descend, pulling over in front of a large group of glass domes. The bright flowers of vine garlands and the shimmer of fluttering colorful birds and insects inside made the domes appear as if they were twinkling with bursts of color.

"What is this place?" I'd assumed he would be taking me to some nice restaurant for brunch or something. This venue looked so much bigger than any of restaurants I'd been to in Voran.

"Come." He climbed out of the aircraft, helping me to get out. His face turned serious, subduing my mood, too.

The doors from the parking platforms slid open, and we entered under a huge glass dome filled with music, flowers, and people—so many people—dressed in the most beautiful, formal wear.

They all turned to us as we walked in, lifting their drink glasses in greeting.

Stopping my gaze at each face individually, I realized I personally knew most if not all of them.

There were the women I'd met at my parenting class, who had since become my very good friends. The employees of my bakery, Earth Girl's Desserts, waved at me from the crowd. Alcus Hecear and a few more members of the Liaison Committee were here, too. As were Governor Drustan and his wife.

Shula gave me a friendly smile when our gazes crossed. She and I had never become close friends, but we held a mutual respect for each other and managed to get along well enough for the sake of the people we cared about in our lives.

Last Christmas, Grevar had informed me that he had officially added "Daisy" to the names of our two boys.

"So everyone would know that they have two mothers," he'd said. "One who gave them birth, and one who became their closest family."

Of course, I'd cried at his words. The fact that he didn't mind his future mighty warriors sporting the word "Daisy" in their names was beyond endearing.

"Are all these people here for us?" I asked Grevar, smiling and waving at everyone in the room.

He didn't get a chance to reply.

"Daisy!" I heard a very familiar female voice. "My baby girl."

"Mom?" My knees nearly buckled, and tears sprung to my eyes when my own mother rushed out of the crowd to greet me. "You're here? How?"

"Grevar got us to Neron." She squeezed me in a hug then kissed my face at least a dozen times.

I managed to glance at Grevar under the shower of her attention. "You did?"

He gave me a wide smile, looking rather smug and proud of himself.

"He is such a charming young man, Daisy. You're so lucky."

"When did you arrive?" I asked Mom, hugging her back.

All of this felt like a dream.

"Oh, just a couple of days ago. We've been staying in a really nice hotel, getting to know this place a little. Grevar wanted it to be a surprise for you."

"Well I *am* surprised," I mumbled, flabbergasted. "So much so, that I'd ask you to pinch me. Except that if it's really a dream I don't want to wake up." I hugged her tighter. "I missed you, mom."

"We all missed you so much, too. How are you feeling, baby?" She patted my belly. "I can't wait to meet my new granddaughter."

"Are you staying here until her birth, then?"

"Of course we are. Oh, Dad is here, too, and Lily with Max and their children. We all are here," she chatted. "This was such an amazing opportunity to fly to another planet to visit you. We all wanted to come. Lily chose to stay up during the flight. She said she got a lot of work done. Max too. The rest of us slept. Look!" She patted her cheeks, with a soft giggle. "I'm five months older, with no extra wrinkles to show for it."

My head was spinning from her chatter. Dad always said I took after her in that, but I didn't think I could ever compete with her speed of talking.

"Where are all of them?" I turned around, looking for other members of my family.

"Lily and Max are over there, by the bar." My sister and her husband had already spotted us and were making their way to us through the crowd. "And Dad?" Mom turned around, too, searching with her gaze. "The last time I saw him, he was playing with Olvar and Zun. Adorable little boys. They made him keep score while they were wrestling…"

"Oh, we won't see him any time soon, then, if the twins have claimed him for themselves." Grevar chuckled.

"And the boys are here, too?" I pivoted his way. "You managed to get them out of school early, without telling me?"

He grinned wider. "It was all a surprise, remember?"

"Right." The amount of planning he'd put into it was astounding. Grevar took everything he did very seriously. He must have approached this like a complex military operation.

His father, the retired General Rufut Kyradus made his way to us through the crowd. "Son. Daughter."

I smiled wide, spotting him, and didn't mind a bit when he grabbed my ears and placed a quick smooch on my face before doing the same to his son.

"Congratulations, children," he said with a serious expression, though his firm mouth quivered a little.

"Thank you, but... Congratulations on what?" I moved my gaze from him to Grevar.

"Merry Christmas." After rummaging in his pocket, Grevar took out a small leather box.

My heart skipped a beat as he lowered himself down to one knee.

"Daisy Grevar Kyradus," he said flipping the lid open to display a rose-gold ring, with a sunny yellow stone inside it. "You're the love of my life. Will you continue being my wife?"

I smiled so wide, my mouth hurt, even as tears rushed to my eyes. So many emotions flooded through me at once. Love. Joy. Happiness.

"Yes." I nodded, wiping at the tears with the back of my hand. "A million times *yes*."

Everyone cheered and clapped.

Slipping the ring on my finger, Grevar got up then took me in his arms.

"I love you." He gave me a tender kiss, pressing me to his chest.

"I love you, too." I kept smiling, melting into his embrace. "You are my dream man, Grevar. You keep making all my dreams come true. Even the ones I didn't know I had."

THE END

Next in My Holiday Tails Series

<u>MY TINY GIANT</u>

During a mission on planet Tragul, I have the misfortune to get stranded with Lieutenant Agan Drankai, the most arrogant prick in the entire alien army of Ravils. I even happen to save his life during the combat. But the big, tough Agan isn't too pleased about being saved by a "tiny" human female.

When he and I end up separated from the rest, we get captured and brought to a secret lab supposedly operated by our allies. A rogue scientist performs an illegal experiment on Agan, which finally allows the haughty lieutenant to get a taste of his own medicine.

The tough guy is now no bigger than my palm.

Did he hate to be saved by a woman before? Now, he literally has to be carried back to his army base by one.

And the safest way for me to do that is to stuff him in my bra.

Despite his small size, Agan's ego remains as big as ever, but so are his confidence, courage, and loyalty. The better I get to know him, the more I find his "little self" growing on me.

COMING JANUARY 2021

More by Marina Simcoe

PARANORMAL ROMANCE

Madame Tan's Freakshow
Call of Water
Madness of the Moon
Power of Rage

Demons, Complete Series
Demon Mine
The Forgotten
Grand Master
The Last Unforgiven - Cursed
The Last Unforgiven - Freed

Stand Alone Novels Set in Demons World
The Real Thing
To Love A Monster

Midnight Coven Author Group
Wicked Warlock (Cursed Coven)

SCIENCE-FICTION ROMANCE

Dark Anomaly Trilogy
Gravity
Power
Explosion

My Holiday Tails
Married To Krampus
My Tiny Giant

Standalone Novels
Experiment
Enduring (Valos Of Sonhadra)

About the Author

MARINA SIMCOE LIKES to write love stories with characters, who may or may not be entirely human, because she firmly believes that our contemporary world could always use a little bit of the extraordinary.

She has lots of fun exploring how her out-of-this-world characters with their own beliefs, values, and aspirations fit into our every-day life.

She lives in Canada with her very own grumpy brute, their three little kids, and a cat, who is definitely out of this world.

For updates on her future books please visit Marina Simcoe Author page on Facebook or www.marinasimcoe.com.

Please Stay in Touch

Newsletter signup: http://eepurl.com/c__RGn
Facebook Readers' Group
Marina's Reading Cave
www.instagram.com/marinasimcoeauthor
www.marinasimcoe.com
www.facebook.com/MarinaSimcoeAuthor/
www.amazon.com/author/marinasimcoe
www.bookbub.com/profile/marina-simcoe
www.goodreads.com/MarinaSimcoe